MIDNIGHT RUN

ROBERT	CHARLES
DE NIRO	GRODIN

A CITY LIGHT FILMS COMPANY Production
A MARTIN BREST FILM "MIDNIGHT RUN"
YAPHET KOTTO · JOHN ASHTON
DENNIS FARINA · JOE PANTOLIANO
Written by GEORGE GALLO
Original Score by DANNY ELFMAN
Executive Producer WILLIAM S. GILMORE
Produced and Directed by MARTIN BREST
A UNIVERSAL PICTURE

A Novel by PAUL MONETTE

Based on a Screenplay by
GEORGE GALLO

GRAFTON BOOKS

A Division of the Collins Publishing Group

LONDON GLASGOW
TORONTO SYDNEY AUCKLAND

Grafton Books
A Division of the Collins Publishing Group
8 Grafton Street, London W1X 3LA

A Grafton UK Paperback Original 1988
This edition published by arrangement with
The Berkley Publishing Group, New York, and
MCA Publishing Rights, a Division of MCA INC.

ISBN 0-586-20520-9

Printed and bound in Great Britain by
Collins, Glasgow

For Craig Rowland,
my Tuscan friend

1

THE '76 OLDS, SNOT green with gray primer splotches, crept slowly along the gritty street, buffeted by a Santa Ana wind. It was past one in the morning, and the asphalt on South Avalon Street still smoldered with the stink of a no-man's-land on permanent red alert. The bloody Watts riots were almost twenty years ago, but South Avalon still had a major chip on its shoulder.

To the dark, lean figure at the wheel of the Olds, everyplace in L.A. was cruising for some kind of fight, even on a nice, dead, smoggy day. But with the Santa Ana blowing, the ions crackling in the upper air, and everything dry to the bone, certain places in the city began to come apart at the seams. It was not a good time to go to the dentist, or be locked in a very small place with a short fuse. No wonder the Indians called them devil winds.

The lean man hung both elbows over the steering wheel. He was slumped like a man who could have been falling asleep, except for the hawklike glitter in his eyes. He didn't at all look like a man who was searching out his way. He'd been here before, one way or another, even if it wasn't always Avalon Street, or even L.A. The shock of dark hair that hooded his brow was predatory, but those

bright obsidian eyes were after something more than game.
Not that he wasn't capable of killing. You couldn't come
this far south on Avalon Street without being ready and
willing.

The Olds passed slowly in and out of gaudy light and
deep shadow as the man peered straight ahead. The flow
of traffic lights, neon bar signs, blue-white streetlamps
washed his intent face with a mercury of shifting colors.
His face was haggard from too little sleep, and he'd long
since given up trying to make it up over the weekend.
He'd long since given up weekends, for that matter.

But for all its tautness and grim determination, Jack
Walsh's face also revealed the tentative play of an antic
smile, as if he was always waiting for the punch line.
Something held the smile in check, but he couldn't keep it
down, not with an all-night talk show babbling in his ear.
A lady from Pacoima was telling in great psychotic detail
that her neighbors across the street were poisoning her
with microwaves, setting up four ovens aimed directly at
her house.

"My husband says they're aliens," she confessed to the
all-night host, "but the car's got Florida plates."

Jack Walsh whipped his head toward the sound of break-
ing glass. On the opposite curb he saw two men squaring
off for a drunken fight in front of a topless bar. A woman
in the doorway screeched at the men, but it wasn't clear if
she wanted them to stop or go for blood. A heroin-thin
Chicana in a white mini and stiletto heels, she stepped to
the curb and shoved at the taller of the two black men.
Jack slowed the Olds for a red light and watched the
scuffle attentively, flipping off the radio as if he'd found
something better.

"Alto! Alto!" the Chicana cried, pushing the taller man
toward his opponent. Both men looked too drunk to fight.
When she couldn't budge her main man, she stalked over

to the other guy and spat in his face. He turned and lumbered away, and the Chicana stood in a fuming rage, the crime of passion evaporating around her.

Then she noticed Walsh watching from the Olds. She marched to the curb. With a flat hand she shaded her eyes from the neon glare and took a belligerent stance. Walsh allowed a slow grin to split his deadpan face. He didn't say a word, but she didn't appear to take it as an insult. For a moment she looked almost vulnerable as she returned the grin with a tentative smile. Then she gave a small shrug, as if to say what can you do. Walsh gave out with a one-note laugh, then the light went green, and he pulled away.

A few blocks down he hung a right off the boulevard and crept through the darkness of a narrow side street. Most of the streetlights had been shot out long ago, and he had to lean out the window to make out numbers on the dim-lit apartment houses. When he pulled the Olds over to the curb, he felt a bottle burst beneath his rear tire. He grunted slightly, as if he'd lost too many tires on streets without any lights. But he seemed pretty certain now he was in the right place.

He pulled an unfiltered Camel cigarette and a Zippo lighter from the pocket of his flannel shirt. He never used the Zippo without appreciating the solid, satisfying click when he opened it. The damn thing leaked a bit, and Walsh always had about him the faint smell of lighter fluid. But it never left his side, not since Benny Hunnible tossed it to him. Benny was built like a linebacker, coarse and foul-mouthed, and was the only friend Walsh had made in his whole twelve-month tour in Nam. Benny had lobbed the Zippo to Walsh about five seconds before a VC land mine exploded under the big man's feet. Walsh could still feel the spray in his own face as he fell to the ground unhurt.

He held the Zippo between his thumb and two fingers and snapped them, flipping the lid. He struck a blue flame and lit the Camel. He took a long drag, then dropped the Zippo back in his pocket, patting it twice for good luck. Through the blue-gray smoke Walsh fixed his gaze on a warped and grungy four-story slum across the way, indistinguishable from the rest of the hulking wrecks that lined the street. For a moment the only light in the car came from the tip of the Camel and the white slits of Walsh's eyes. He was utterly still on the surface, but beneath the gunmetal stare pressure was building up. Jack Walsh lived sometimes in the hair-trigger second of taut suspension just before an explosion. His eyes were ground zero.

He glanced down at his watch, a tarnished old Timex, well-worn and battered as the Olds. There was nothing new in Walsh's life. It was time. He took a last drag on the Camel, flicked it into the street, and pushed open the car door with his shoulder. As he rolled out he pulled a .45 from the holster under his jacket and checked the magazine. Loaded. He slipped the gun back and took a deep breath of the night wind, like a prairie dog about to howl.

His quick eyes took in the whole street as he trotted toward the tenement. He glanced at the bank of mailboxes in front of the building, all of them ripped open and cankered with rust. Nobody lived here, as far as the post office knew, but then nobody wrote a lot of letters.

Inside he smelled mildew and urine. Bars of security grating covered a few of the downstairs apartment doors, and none had less than three locks. In this neighborhood you never knew if they were locking something in or out. Except for the muffled sound of sitcom laughter, the place was grimly quiet. Walsh's eyes darted continually—a reflex—as he moved up the first flight of stairs, not making a sound.

The landing and hallway on the second floor were littered with trash, as if nobody had the strength to fling it downstairs. A burst mattress slouched against one wall. Across the wall was scrawled "JESUS SUCKS," with what looked like a kid's crayons. A real class toilet, Walsh decided. His foot knocked an empty Thunderbird bottle, which rolled and clattered down the stairs behind him. "Shit," he muttered.

A dog barked from somewhere down on the first floor, a futile, hysterical bark, as if it hadn't been out for days. Then it was quiet again, and Walsh mounted to the third floor. The overhead light was jaundice yellow as he squinted at the numbers on the doors. He stopped at 3-C, put an ear to the door. Nothing. He slipped a leather packet from the pocket of his jeans. Inside it was a neat row of lockpicks. He drew one out with the deadly calm of a surgeon selecting a scalpel, then bent to ease it into the tumblers.

Dammit, he dropped it. The thin pick fell among the dust balls on the doorjamb, and Walsh crouched to his knees to retrieve it. Then suddenly—BLAMM! And the upper half of the door exploded into splinters, exactly where his head had been a half-second before. Walsh bounced on his ass as shotgun pellets sprayed the corridor. "Aw fuck," he groaned as he yanked out the .45 and hunkered into a crouch.

He didn't have to open the door to get a good look into 3-C. As he peered above the edge of the smoking hole he saw a burly young black man scrambling out the window onto a fire escape. In an instant Walsh kicked open what was left of the door and leaped across the grungy apartment, passing a freaked-out tabby cat whose hair stood on end. Walsh ducked his head out the window frame and saw his prey clanging up the iron stairs to the roof.

Walsh slung himself out the window and rocketed up the fire escape. He reached the gravel roof just in time to see the black man leap across the four-story drop to the next tenement. Walsh made a growling noise in his throat, as if he was getting a bit too old for the high jump, but he bounded across the roof and took the leap without looking down. He could feel his knees protest as he landed on the second roof, which only made him more grimly determined. ''Bouchet!'' he hollered at the fleeing man with the shotgun.

Bouchet didn't even turn around but gathered his muscular frame for the jump to the next building. Walsh was so pissed now that he sailed across the wider gap without even thinking. Bouchet was only twenty feet ahead of him now. The black man glanced over his shoulder, stunned that Walsh was still on his tail. Ahead was a chasm fifteen feet wide. He had no other choice as he pumped his legs and sprang from the edge, soaring across the alley and landing with a tumble on the next roof. Walsh braced himself to follow, a delirious picture in his mind of the two of them vaulting the city roof by roof till morning. Bouchet was already scrambling to his feet as Walsh kicked free and flew the long, empty distance . . . and just missed.

He caught the ledge of the roof with his armpits, feeling as if his shoulders were going to rip away from his body. Through clenched teeth he gave a murderous grunt. The rotted ledge began to break free. Face contorting with strain, by pure will alone, Walsh hoisted himself over the top just as the ledge coping fell away beneath him. His face slid across the rough tar paper of the roof, and by the time he leaped to his feet he could see Bouchet drop down a fire escape at the far end of the bilding.

Walsh hauled ass, so sore he couldn't figure what *didn't* hurt anymore. As he reached the fire escape, the black man stopped on the landing below and opened fire with the shotgun. Walsh ducked, then barreled down anyway, clanging after Bouchet. The black man reached the bottom and started tearing down the alley, Walsh a bare beat behind him. Bouchet was panicked now, and he whirled around and blasted the shotgun again. Walsh dove behind a dumpster as the buckshot ricocheted.

Suddenly, out of nowhere, two brilliant headlights appeared at the end of the alley. As Walsh came around the dumpster, some deep instinct in him sounded an alarm. The headlights roared toward them down the narrow concrete corridor. Frantically Bouchet tried to flatten himself against the side of the building, but the car sideswiped him and spun him completely around.

The black man shrieked as he skidded onto the concrete, hunching his elbows to protect his face. The car, a liver-colored gunboat Caddie, careened to a stop, and a stunted, pudding-faced man uncoiled himself from the driver's seat. A stingy moustache flaked with dandruff barely covered his upper lip. His toupee had always reminded Walsh of a veal cutlet.

Walsh slapped dirt from the knees of his pants, then ambled over to the car, his glittering eyes fixed on the driver. No telling what a bad Santa Ana condition can blow your way. Both men eyed each other, ignoring for the moment the terrified punk who huddled against the pavement, not daring to move or whimper. A smirk congealed on the new man's face. His nostrils dilated slightly as the sneer revealed a two-bit set of false teeth.

"He's mine, Walsh."

"What the hell are you doin', Dorfler?" Walsh demanded, looking down at the Caddie contemptuously. They were suddenly two salesmen, staking turf. Walsh looked like a man who was trapped in a tough and ratty enterprise. Dorfler looked as if he'd paid somebody off to be there.

Dorfler moved to the black man huddled on the pavement and nudged him with the toe of one shoe, turning him over. "Get lost, Jack," he called over his shoulder.

"Fuck you, he's yours," countered Walsh with a hoot of derision. "Moscone assigned him to me."

Dorfler planted a foot on Bouchet's chest, then twisted it back and forth as if squashing an insect, or grinding out a cigarette butt. The black man gave a yelp of protest. What Dorfler lacked in finesse he made up for with pointless force and dim, impulsive behavior. "Well, you better go straighten that out with Moscone," he said. "I'm collectin' the money."

"Goddamn you, Dorfler," spat out Walsh, his face not a foot from the veal cutlet. "I nearly lost my ass up there, trying to get this dude. F'get it, he's mine."

Dorfler whipped a .45 from his doubleknit jacket. Pointed it in Walsh's face. "Back off, Jack. I'm takin' him."

On the pavement Bouchet looked up at the two men in bewildered disbelief. "Hey, what the fuck's goin' on?" he asked in a wounded tone.

Walsh grinned from ear to ear, not so much as blinking at the gun. "Maxie, Maxie," he said, clucking his tongue, "why are we fightin'? You and me are friends since grammar school or somethin'."

"Nothin' personal, Jack. Guy's worth fifteen hundred. Now get lost."

He held the gun more coldly, and Walsh backed off with his scuffed hands raised. Dorfler held his gunman's stance till Walsh had backed to the end of the alley, where it spewed out onto South Avalon. Satisfied at last, Dorfler turned to the black man, so he didn't quite see Jack Walsh break into a sprint around the corner. Dorfler yanked Bouchet to his feet and reached in the Caddie for a pair of handcuffs.

"Hey, you guys ain't cops," protested Bouchet, still dazed from eating the pavement.

"No, actually we're musicians," Dorfler replied dryly. "Now get in the fuckin' car."

He clamped the cuffs on the black man's wrists, pulled open the front door of the Caddie, and shoved Bouchet into the passenger seat. As he slammed the door, he heard a bottle crash behind the car, toward the end of the alley where Walsh had disappeared onto South Avalon. "That you, Walsh?" he called suspiciously. He pulled the .45 from his jacket and took a tentative step toward the sound.

Behind him Jack Walsh grinned, breathing heavily from running around the building. "No, Maxie," he declared dryly, slipping behind the wheel of the Caddie, "I'm actually right over here." And as Dorfler whipped around in stunned surprise, Walsh slung the shift into drive and screeched away past the dumpster, yanking the door shut as he peeled around the corner.

Dorfler was so apoplectic he didn't move at all for a minute. Just his lips began to twitch, like a fish gulping for air. A sound like a whinny emerged from his mouth. He looked back and forth down the alley, as if he had a sudden horror that somebody might have seen him. Then he began to roar.

Walsh slowed the liver-spotted Cadillac and took the turn off Grand Street into the parking lot of the L.A. County Jail. He pulled in between two concrete stanchions and took a parking ticket from the automatic feed. The wooden gate yawned open, but Walsh only inched the car halfway through. He turned to Bouchet beside him, still in handcuffs.

"Fasten your seat belt, and open your door," Walsh ordered. Puzzled but obedient, Bouchet did as he was told. Walsh did the same on the driver's side, methodical and in no hurry, as if he were setting up an elaborate chess move. Satisfied that the doors were open now like wings, a peaceful half-grin on his face, he threw the Caddie into reverse and backed up full throttle. The doors exploded against the stanchions with an agonized groan, ripping them from their hinges.

"All right!" shouted Bouchet gleefully.

Walsh slammed the car into drive and wheeled in a tight half-circle, racing for the wrong end of the exit. A red sign gaped above the shark's row of metal teeth along the pavement: SEVERE TIRE DAMAGE! DO NOT PRO-CEED! Walsh shot a quick glance at the black man, as if to get a second opinion.

"Go for it!' exulted Bouchet.

Walsh beat the accelerator pedal to the floor, and the tires exploded like a terrorist attack as the Caddie rocketed through. Dorfler's car was limping and careening now, but Walsh didn't let up on the gas. He sailed the Caddie forward into a parking space and slammed a brick wall, collapsing the front end and springing the hood like a jack-in-the-box. Bouchet applauded beside him in his handcuffs.

"You know, somehow I don't think this space is safe enough," said Walsh. "Wouldn't want to get sideswiped, ya know." And he threw it into reverse again and backed like crazy through an expanse of empty spaces till he slammed the opposite wall, crumpling the Caddie's space-ship fins. As the crippled car rocked in place, Bouchet whistling with drunken glee, the bumper fell off like an afterthought.

Somehow the parking lot happened to be completely empty of onlookers in the predawn light. The sheriff's men in the County Jail were used to their crime and destruction taking place a little further afield. But a carload of teenag-ers cruising down Grand caught nearly the whole spectacle of Walsh's demolition derby. They watched dumbfounded while the Caddie fell apart, then sped away as soon as the wreck had settled, fearing guilt by association.

Bouchet was still pounding the dashboard with uproarious delight as Walsh turned and smiled at him serenely. The black man was younger than Walsh had thought, barely in his twenties. The hint of a goatee shadowed his otherwise smooth face. Walsh felt an unwelcome and disquieting pang of sympathy. Bouchet's natural laughter died away as the bounty hunter gazed at him. Then it was quiet: neither man had forgotten what they were doing here.

"This is where we get out," Walsh said gruffly, avoiding the boy's eyes.

They walked across the deathly quiet of the lot and in through the rear entrance. In the doorway, Walsh released one cuff from Bouchet's wrist and cuffed it to his own. The black man suddenly looked dwarfed and rattled. "All I did," he pleaded to Walsh, "was come home and Ray was sleepin' with my old lady. So I shot him, right? What's the big deal?"

Walsh pushed open the heavy glass door and led his prisoner in. They turned down a wide, institutional-green corridor. Their shoes on the splattered linoleum produced that sick hollow echo peculiar to county buildings, especially late at night. The long stretches of an airport had a certain melancholy at 4 A.M., but they still gave the feeling that people were on their way somewhere. Most people here at County had already gotten to where they were going. Nothing would ever change much for the guys who got hauled in on the graveyard shift.

Walsh gave a sidelong glance at Monroe Bouchet, wondering how the kid fit into that grim continuum. Would this be the first in a lifetime of going nowhere fast? Walsh knew he wasn't supposed to think about it at all.

Bouchet droned on in his own defense. "Then I hear on the TV that the dude was *lucid*. Hey, man, I didn't do no lucid shit to him. I swear."

Walsh felt another uncomfortable wrench of sympathy

in his gorge. Yeah, Bouchet shot the guy all right. But there wasn't a soul in County who gave a damn if the kid knew what "lucid" meant. Poor bastard. "Lucid means like he was coherent," Walsh said evenly, patient as a schoolteacher. "Makin' sense when he talked. That's lucid."

A gleam flashed in Bouchet's eyes. "Shit," he hooted, "dude wasn't lucid *before* I shot him. Maybe I made him lucid, huh?" Both men laughed with equal gusto now, a couple of pals sharing a private joke.

Ahead of them a tall, angular black woman in a heavy sweater bent over a wringer-bucket, struggling to free the strands of a filthy, tangled mop. She almost pulled the bucket over, and brown water slopped on the just-mopped floor. It was all pretty useless, washing the floor at County. Walsh could feel by the subtlest tug on the cuffs that Bouchet would have given her a hand to free the mop. As they passed her she gave them a weary look, glancing down instinctively at the cuffs. It was clear who was leading whom. She glared at the young black man with a look of disgust and reprimand. Who knew how many sons and nephews she'd watched walk into County? She smiled at Walsh, ignoring Bouchet.

As Walsh and his captive came into the booking room, Walsh automatically noted that it was a quiet night. Only a few prisoners milled about with their exhausted lawyers. Obviously not a full moon tonight. On a bench beside the booking desk was a middle-aged woman with matted red hair. Her dirty feet splayed over rubber thongs. She rocked slowly back and forth in a constant, slow "yes" nod. She seemed more loiterer than criminal, and she certainly didn't have a lawyer.

Behind the booking window a cop with the mealy gray eyes and skin of an all-night coffee drinker watched a two-inch Sony. His head looked as if it were held in a sort of vise by the steady beam of the tube. Walsh jangled his key ring to get the cop's attention, then bent to release Bouchet. "Hey, Gooch, I got a delivery," Walsh announced in a clipped voice. "Monroe Bouchet." He slid the booking papers through the window like a claim check in a pawnshop.

"Give you any trouble?" drawled Sergeant Gooch— just a question, no special malice. But he didn't acknowledge Bouchet's presence in any way, not so much as a glance.

"Nah, he was real cooperative," Walsh replied as he rubbed Bouchet's wrist between his own hands. A bluish depression surrounded the silky coffee skin where Dorfler's cuffs had cut into the flesh. "A regular charmer," Walsh added, grinning at Bouchet. He meant it, and Bouchet knew he meant it. Have a good life, kid.

"Take care of yourself, Monroe."

"Hey, you, too, man," retorted the black man cheerfully. "Next time let's get us an El Dorado, huh?" And he winked broadly at the bounty hunter, no hard feelings at all. Walsh held the look in his mind for almost a full minute after Gooch had led the big man away to the holding cell beyond the book room.

2

ON VIGNES STREET, across the way from County, a peaked little carnival of bail bond offices were clustered together on two short blocks. A couple of them were prefab bungalows, of the kind used to palm off cruddy housing developments. Bold signs teetered on the roofs of the rickety buildings, some of them sideshow neon, gassy colors scribbled across the early morning light.

As Walsh came out of the jailhouse and headed for the bondsmen's midway, the light in the sky reminded him of deep indigo watercolor stroked in layers on spongy paper. He always loved the sense of privacy—of newness—that he felt on those rare mornings when he managed to be awake. The Santa Anas had wrung out every impurity from the air, and the city itself was a bracing sight, snapped to attention. Even the bullshit he was about to walk through wasn't going to wreck this morning for Jack Walsh. He couldn't wait to treat himself to a big truck-stop breakfast . . . *after* he picked up his fifteen hundred dollars.

"Moscone" was the oldest name in L.A. bail bonds. Fifty years ago it was probably a single extended family, but now the three or four Moscones who ran competing operations didn't seem to have the slightest kinship with each other. But then, there's not a lot of camaraderie in a business that trades on shame, and the waste and wreckage of lives.

Eddie Moscone's bond office was the bungalow type, flamingo pink, with sliding glass doors in the front wall and a wooden deck outside. To Walsh it always had the faint rancid look of a Reno wedding chapel. The sliding door didn't slide. Walsh had to use his shoulder to heave it open, grunting slightly as his muscles remembered the rooftop chase. Inside, he shivered in the cadaverous chill of the mildewed air conditioning.

The whole bungalow was hip-deep in jail papers and pointless clutter. Thin, cheap pressboard divided the room into three shoulder-high cubicles. In the general reception area, about ten by fourteen, a figure slouched behind a fully spread *L.A. Times*. Two cracked and curled black shoes, white socks with bracelets of dust, and the frayed cuffs of a pair of very bad pants stuck out from beneath the paper and rested on the desk.

"I just dropped off Bouchet," Walsh announced to the back of the classifieds. "Where's Moscone?"

The well-read man lowered his paper and stared at Walsh with a look of disbelief. "You mean, you finally caught somebody, Jack?" The man's round, shapeless face was pocked by what must have been terminal acne as a kid. He kept wrinkling his nose, an unconscious tic, as though he was always aborting a sneeze.

"Jerry, is he in or what?" Walsh asked wearily. Usually he asked Jerry what stunk on the bottom of his shoe, but not today. He had too much on his mind, and his shoulder hurt like hell.

Jerry didn't answer the question but disappeared behind the paper again. "Says here that eleven percent of people, in the course of dreaming, are aware of that fact while they're in the dream state. Isn't that inneresting?"

Walsh could get real tired of this. He reached both hands to the open newspaper and ripped it neatly down the seam, revealing Jerry, who blinked at him impassively. "Where is he, Jerry?"

Dumbly Jerry still held up the two severed pieces of his *Times*. Clearly, banter wasn't his strong suit. But before the stakes could escalate further, Eddie Moscone bobbed in from the cubicle next to Jerry's, all nervous energy and quick, skittish smiles. He beamed at Walsh like a long-lost son. "Hey, buddy, why didn't you tell me you were out here?"

He finished rolling his shoulders into a cheap plaid sport coat and extended a hand moist as a veal chop. Instead of shaking his hand, Walsh stuffed the booking slip in Moscone's palm. The bondsman stared at it delightedly, this man who juggled cash and clients and a thousand lies at once. He jutted his neck and chin forward, as if trying to fit into a too small collar.

"Fabulous, Jack, fabulous," he said. "Bouchet was twelve hundred, right?" Then he shot a snarling look at Jerry, who still hadn't lowered the torn newspaper. "This ain't the public library, ya know. Get off your ass and file this shit," he ordered, gesturing around at the blizzard of paper.

"No, fifteen," Walsh corrected patiently.

"Oh, yeah, right," Moscone replied, running a hand through his thick black hair, the pride of his Saracen bloodlusting forebears. "Look, I was just going over to Denny's to catch the grand-slam breakfast. They start servin' at six-thirty. Real nice bacon, ya know?"

"You got my fifteen hundred, Eddie?" Walsh had been through this so many times that he didn't even raise his voice. He was on automatic pilot.

"Well, of course I do." Moscone looked suddenly hurt, his pouchy eyes like a basset hound's. "Did you think I was gonna stiff you, Jack?'' His lips parted in a whining smile, a rictus of friendly disbelief.

''You, Eddie? Never.'' Walsh put a big hand on Moscone's shoulder and stared directly at him, while his own face grew dangerously immobile.

''Jack Walsh is the best in the business,'' purred Moscone. ''That's what I always say—ain't that right, Jerry? Come on, Jack, let me buy you some breakfast.''

''I don't eat breakfast,'' Walsh replied tartly, still thinking of the truck-stop hot cakes he planned to eat alone.

''Then have an early lunch.'' Moscone spread his hands in a gesture of sweeping largess. Then he barked over his shoulder at Jerry, ''Watch the phones!''

Not for the first time, Walsh reflected how Moscone could only be at your feet or your throat, as Churchill once observed about the Germans. Moscone struggled with the sliding door, which stuck in the track and made him grumble to Jerry to fix the goddamned thing. But in the next second he was all smiles again, as he guided Walsh out into the vivid morning air. The first streaks of the sun were bright yellow on the royal palms which clattered overhead in the still-brisk air of the dying Santa Ana. Moscone was absolutely ebullient, bursting with morning cheer as though he were just about to start a sunrise service.

''You'll never guess who I ran into,'' Walsh interjected flatly. ''While I was takin' in Bouchet.''

''Who's that?''

''Max Dorfler.''

''No!'' retorted the other, eyes wide and dancing in startled disbelief. ''Funny how the guy keeps poppin' up, huh?''

''Yeah, hysterical. I fuckin' laughed all the way to County.''

Moscone's voice suddenly dropped an octave, as if he

was just about to announce he had cancer. "Jack, I'm not going to bullshit you, babe," he said. Walsh began to make a sound in his throat like a man trying to swallow a pineapple. "I got a little problem right now."

"Stop right there, Eddie." Walsh craned his neck and looked up and down the street. Moscone was bewildered. "You got a newsstand around here anywhere?" Moscone was totally confused now. He shrugged his shoulders helplessly. "See, I need to go buy me a copy of *Playboy*," Walsh continued smoothly, then looked directly at the bondsman. " 'Cause when I'm being jerked off, I like to have somethin' to look at."

"Hey, Jack, you don't trust me or somethin'?" Moscone put a hand to his chest in a truly operatic gesture.

"How come I think I've been through this before, Eddie? How come I'm so sure you're about to tell me you don't got my fifteen hundred?"

Moscone's eyebrows lifted in triumph. He seemed as if he would burst with some kind of secret. "Jack, I got somethin' better than fifteen hundred. All for you, babe."

Jack Walsh groaned. It was worse than he thought.

The Denny's in Death Valley was pretty much the same as the one down the street from Moscone's Bail Bonds, only on Vignes Street they got mangier coyotes raiding the dumpster. The orange vinyl seats and boomerang counter, sterile and loud at the same time, were as blank here as on any freeway off ramp. Only a few of the tables were occupied, since the all-night crowd had finally slunk home and the ones on their way to work hadn't stumbled in yet. Nobody else quite seemed to have Eddie Moscone's eagerness about the grand-slam breakfast.

Walsh ordered *a la carte* steak and eggs, not on the grand-slam part of the menu, and relished Moscone's wince at every special request and side order. The Korean waitress seemed to relish Walsh's creative ordering. A first-generation immigrant, Walsh figured, and her English was probably as impish as her eyes. "You want anything else?" she asked him, a half-grin coming into the wind chime of her voice. Walsh couldn't help but hold her eyes as long as she would let him. She was letting him.

Impatiently Moscone barked his grand-slam order and dismissed Miss Korea with a wave. He hunched across the table, his eyebrows dancing, and spoke in a hushed voice. "You know who Jonathan Mardukas is?"

Walsh nodded carefully. "The Duke? Yeah, I know who he is."

"So what do you know?"

Walsh tapped a Camel on the table and lit it with the Zippo. Moscone did not appear to appreciate the fluidity of Walsh's Zippo technique. "He's that accountant that embezzled a couple mill from some Vegas wise guy and gave it all to charity." Walsh had read all about it in the papers: how some ballsy little pencil pusher had ripped off one of the fat-cat emperors of Vegas, the "Il Duce" of wise guys. Walsh smiled to recall the incident. He had reason to feel quite tickled about it.

"That's pretty good, Jack, only it wasn't a couple mill, it was fifteen. And it wasn't just some wise guy, it was Jimmy Serano." Moscone's voice grew even more hushed as he said the name, as if fearful he might have engaged the evil eye.

Walsh could feel the skin on his scalp tighten. Yeah, he knew it was Serano, all right. But all he said was, "I can read a newspaper."

"Well, I don't want to dredge up the past," retorted Moscone, purring again with barely disguised pleasure, "but wasn't Serano the guy that ran you out of Chi when he was running things back there? Must be eight, ten years, huh?"

"He didn't run me out," Walsh said tightly.

"Sure, sure . . ." Quick as a shrew to smell blood, Moscone moved in for the two-shot. "You left being a cop to do this bounty shit. Chicago police prob'ly had lousy benefits, right?"

"What's the point, Eddie?" There was a dare in Walsh's tone now. The point had better be now, or something was going to break, like Moscone's face.

"The point, Jack, is twenty-five thousand bucks. See, I bailed the accountant out. Only somebody forgot to tell me who he was. If I knew, I never would've put up the bond." As Moscone shook his head with weary disgust, Jack Walsh perked up. Moscone was usually the one who did the screwing and cheating. "I mean, shit," continued the bondsman, "it would only be a matter of time before Serano vanished the guy from the planet. And then, guess what? I'm out my four-hundred-fifty grand."

Well, bless his little black heart, Walsh thought. "You're out four-five-oh on Mardukas?"

"Oh, no, Jack. That's just temporary."

"Temporary how? Sounds like the guy's in the river dancin' in cement shoes."

Moscone shot him an easy grin as he dumped three packets of Equal in his coffee. "Temporary because I got you, Jack. And you're going to find him and bring him back."

"I don't bring back dead people, Eddie." Walsh could feel his mind veer into the past, where a hundred dead men in Chicago proved how quick and thorough Serano could be. Walsh didn't want to remember any of it.

"That's what I'm tellin' ya, Jack. He ain't dead. He sends Jimmy Serano postcards from all over, telling him what a great time he's havin' with Serano's money." Walsh grinned in spite of himself, as Moscone's eyes took a quick paranoid sweep of the room, as if Serano had a goon under every table.

"How much time you got left?" asked Walsh, an unconcealed mockery in his tone.

Moscone looked suddenly very queasy, and Walsh registered that, for the first time today, the little rodent was about to tell the truth. "Friday night I default and have to eat the four-fifty." Moscone spilled it all at once, as if it were one long, ghastly word, as if he muttered it in his sleep at night. Walsh realized how rarely anybody saw Moscone the way he did now, without any bullshit. Moscone was always so busy trying to pull something. He never stopped the bobbing and weaving long enough for anyone to see the finger-bitten small businessman sitting at the desk in his head, always fretting, the columns never quite adding up. Right now Walsh was looking at a very shaken man, and the curl of sympathy soured his chest again like heartburn.

Walsh stood up abruptly. "That's five days, Eddie. You gotta be kiddin'. Forget it, huh? *You* go find him." He gestured to Miss Korea that Moscone was taking care of the check for the food that hadn't arrived yet. Oh, yes, Walsh was on his way out of there, no question about it. Good-bye, Charlie.

Moscone sprang up from the booth, making a farting noise on the orange plastic. He gripped Walsh's arm and spoke pleadingly. "Hear me out, Jack. Can't you see I'm in jam city?" Walsh winced slightly at Moscone's attempt to sound hip. Why did losers always lose in front of him? "Jack, I'll give you fifty grand if you'll do it."

Walsh started for the door. "I've got to chase you like a fuckin' rabbit just to get my fifteen hundred. No dice, Eddie."

Moscone slid sideways out of the booth and blocked him, dancing in place with a wheedling crouch. The guy was shameless. "Jack, Jack, how can you do this to me? If you don't go find Mardukas, I'll be out of business." His voice grew higher and more desperate. "I can't absorb this kind of loss. Think of my kids, Jack."

Walsh glanced around at the A.M. crowd, wondering what they were making of this spectacle. Amazingly enough, most of them went on eating their grand slams, hardly paying any attention at all. No doubt they were used to a fair amount of delirium in a place that was only a stone's throw from County. As long as there weren't any weapons out, they were all prepared to ignore a little hysteria. Walsh turned back to Moscone, who waited plaintively, wringing his hands like a high-school Shylock.

"I'll do it for a hundred grand," Walsh said with an impassive shrug.

"A hundred grand!" Moscone fairly shrieked in horror. At the sound of the dollar amount, Miss Korea looked up from a huddle of waitresses by one of the coffee warmers. Maybe there were going to be weapons, after all. "Are you out of your mind?" Moscone bellowed accusingly. He hopped up and down in front of Walsh like Rumpelstiltskin. "This is an easy gig, Jack. It's a midnight run, for Christ's sake." He clutched Walsh's sleeve. "C'mon, Jack, siddown. Let's talk about this. Please. Be my friend."

Jack Walsh faltered just for a second. It certainly wasn't that Eddie Moscone was his friend. Perhaps he was getting sick of the heated scene in the middle of the restaurant. Perhaps he just wanted his breakfast. But he sat down in the booth again, and Moscone, with a sigh of relief, followed suit. "If you want me for a job this big," Walsh declared quietly, "then you pay me what's right. Maybe you haven't noticed, Eddie, but I'm tired of getting shot at."

"Jack, the guy's an accountant!" Moscone laughed at

the sheer absurdity of it. "He's not going to shoot you. Just put a paper bag over his head, hit him with a rubber hose, and stick him on an airplane. Like I said, it's just a midnight run."

The most important decisions of Walsh's life had always been made in a split second. He knew, of course, when something wasn't working out, but he was the type who hung on. With Gail he'd known for a long time, but he'd thought that just a little more effort, little more time, little more something. Just hang on and work so hard you don't have to think about it too much. Problem was, he was thinking about the bounty hunting all the time, and he'd had it up to his eyeballs. Sick of the small-time hoods, the bondsmen, the booking clerks, the whole scumbag lot. It was past time for one of those split-second maneuvers, and he knew it.

"You heard what I said," Walsh replied precisely, locking eyes with Moscone. "I'll do it for a hundred grand, and then I'm out of this business forever." Now his voice took on a flinty edge, as if he would drive the kind of tough bargain that had eluded him all his life. "And I want a contract, Eddie. I want it in writing. A hundred grand, and I'll have the Duke here by Friday night."

Moscone darted a look left and right, as if he still thought he could talk his way out of it, but the gesture was mostly a formality. Finally he looked at Walsh, whose eyes had not wavered, and he nodded slowly. "You got yourself a deal."

Then, as if she'd been waiting on the sidelines till the negotiations were done, Miss Korea arrived with the breakfasts. She smiled puckishly at Walsh as she laid his toast in front of him, and he reached up and helped her balance a dish that teetered on her forearm. As she turned to serve Moscone his grand-slam special, Walsh noticed the delicate way her hair was gathered into a comb, just above the hollow at the back of her neck. What was it about a woman's neck that was so exquisite and incorruptible? So sexy and childlike at the same time?

Now she bent and poured them each more coffee, bowing slightly, as if some elaborate unconscious memory still lingered from an ancient ceremony. She didn't look ridiculous at all in her Denny's white-and-orange. As she moved to leave the table, Walsh shot her the same grin he'd given the Chicana on the sidewalk on South Avalon. Two grins in one night were more than Walsh had allowed himself in months. He'd almost forgotten how good it was to take the time to notice a beautiful woman. He suddenly had the very unoriginal thought that they were probably all over the place, if he would only bother to look more.

The grin was still on his face as he turned to Moscone once again. The bondsman was scarfing up his eggs and bacon and hot cakes all at once, as if the Saracen hordes might sweep down at any minute. "So," said Jack Walsh, reaching for a Camel, "you think I could have my fifteen hundred now?"

3

RAMPART DIVISION HEADQUARTERS whined with a din like the trading floor of a stock exchange. Jack Walsh, hair still damp from the shower, with an actual tie around his neck, wound his way through the welter of jangling telephones and the collapsing palisades of files and paper work on almost every desk. The room was huge and throbbed with fluorescent light, much bigger than the detectives' room where Walsh had done his time in Chicago. His eyes swept the room with twenty-twenty clarity, but he felt it more than he saw it—a palpable energy that slammed him with a broadside wallop.

He tried not to resent the cops buzzing around him, most of them crazed to finish forty things before watch roll call. Some were as old-school as he was, but there were a lot of punks, too. Punks was what the Chi cops used to call the new breed: urban, painfully young, flashy as car dealers, working narcotics or vice undercover. Hell, would he really like to be back in a place like this? Barely skimming the avalanche of dope. The metastasizing cancer of the soul that eats at cops, till the whole world looks like "us" and "them." Not to mention the interdepartment idiocy, the obscenely high divorce and suicide rates. Would he really want to be pulled apart again like that, for twenty-two grand a year?

In a hot second he would.

A hand clamped down on his shoulder, and a raucous whiskey voice interrupted his reverie. "I was just saying to myself that this has been the worst day since the Manson killings, all I need now is Jack Walsh to appear." Walsh turned to the bloodshot grin of Dave Hammond, chief of detectives. "And look what blows in, right on schedule." He cuffed the back of Walsh's head affectionately. Hammond's face had no angles or planes, just a wide-open simplicity. No signs of great intelligence, either, but his loyalty made up for it in spades.

"Dave, I need a favor."

"Yeah, what do you need?" mocked Hammond. "A case of Jack Daniels? That's what I need, too."

"Can you get me the booking slip for a guy named Jonathan Mardukas?"

Hammond nodded. "I'll get you a copy."

"No, Dave," Walsh retorted impatiently, "I need to see the original."

Hammond's eyes widened slightly. "Pardon me, Lord Dudley. Copies were good enough for the FBI."

Walsh made a slight hissing sound as he sucked in a breath. "They're lookin' for him, too?"

"The guy's wanted in seven states," Hammond replied dryly, jerking his head for Walsh to follow him.

As they zigzagged their way through the brawling chaos of the detectives' room, Walsh reflected that Hammond was one of the few who knew about the old trouble in Chicago, and yet he never once alluded to it in any way. The guy had class. He was built like a zoo bear, kind of overfed, and he'd once told Walsh that he didn't "cuss." And he meant it: he wasn't being a wimp or a good Catholic. He just never thought to talk that way, in spite of a hundred detectives all around him who could curl your hair with invective.

They headed downstairs to Records, the domain of Sgt. Beatrice Inkersoll, a wide-bodied, good-natured broad, broad being her word. Women's Liberation had nothing to teach her. "Big Bea" often referred to herself in the third person as "a broken-down old broad with a lot of mileage but pretty good tread." Her flirting with anything with fly buttons was shameless, crude, and constant, though in fact she'd spent her real life putting two boys through college single-handedly.

Big Bea's eyes narrowed as she flipped quickly through the master file, searching for the arrest record on Jonathan Mardukas, a.k.a. "The Duke." She gave Hammond the file coordinates and waved them into the file room, adding a ribald comment about Walsh's rear end. Walsh wiggled his hips as he followed Hammond, sending Big Bea into gales of laughter.

Hammond slid open a file cabinet and fished out a manila folder. He yawned the folder open and offered it to Walsh, who rifled among the papers till he found a small booking card, about four by six. Walsh glanced at the front, crossed his fingers and drew in his breath, and flipped the card over. Scribbled on the back was a phone number, starting with 212. Walsh grinned. This was the fun part: bit by bit the picture becoming clear, till Walsh could *feel* him out there somewhere.

"What's that?" asked Hammond, peering at the scribble.

"The number he called after he was arrested," Walsh replied casually. Elementary, my dear Hammond. He rifled his pockets for a pencil and paper and transferred the number from the booking card. "Two-one-two. Looks like I'm going to New York."

As Walsh came trotting down the steps of the Rampart

station into the midmorning glare of Beverly Boulevard, a
very large black man watched him through steel-rimmed
sunglasses. The black man stood at the curb by a car that
screamed its unmarked status. His wide, heavy face showed
no curved smile lines anywhere, though a short, deep
vertical fret ran straight up and down between his eyebrows, giving him a perpetual scowl. Everything about
Alonso Mosely, like the blade-sharp creases in his navy
blue suit, ran straight up and down.

Walsh walked east on Beverly, trying to decide if he
needed to go home and pack first. Then he figured he
might as well take off fast and clean and pick up whatever
he needed on the way. He didn't need much anymore,
except that hundred grand. He hadn't gone fifty yards
before Mosely was standing in front of him, eyes about a
foot from his face. There were only two things that Walsh
was slightly phobic about. One was having his wrists held,
which made him explode like a madman; the other was
somebody barging into his personal space uninvited.

He returned the black man's stare and said, "Excuse
me," but not very politely, as if the next thing he might do
was sever the guy's windpipe.

"You Jack Walsh?" demanded Mosely.

Something prickled across Walsh's scalp. "Do I know
you?" he retorted with a grisly smile. Then he suddenly
snapped his fingers and jutted his chin out. "Wait, I got it.
Didn't I take your cousin in last week?"

"I don't think so. My cousin's a gynecologist."

"No shit. I always get kinda nervous when a gynecologist can palm a basketball." Walsh was starting to enjoy
this thing, but the black man had no imagination. He
reached in his suit-coat pocket to pull out identification.
Walsh stepped around him and started to walk.

When Mosely stepped in front of him again, Walsh
blew. "Get the fuck out of my way!" he screamed at the

bigger man, shoving him aside. This was what Gail used to call "bananas," and it scared the bejesus out of anyone who knew him, the lightning change, the savage rage. It had saved his butt more than once. But just now, three other men as big as Mosely, with the same knife creases in their suits, sprang out of nowhere and pinned Walsh.

They formed a phalanx of blue suits and hustled Walsh down the sidewalk toward a dun-green Plymouth. Happily Walsh knew when to relax. He was pissed, not crazy or stupid. So skillfully had the blue suits grabbed him that the straggling pedestrians along the sidewalk hardly stopped to notice. As one of them got into the Plymouth next to Mosely, Walsh was crammed into the back seat between the other two. All four wore sunglasses with dark green lenses. Walsh sat in silence as they stared him down.

Mosely locked his massive arm and shoulder over the top of the seat. "Inspector Mosely. FBI."

"I figured that part out," retorted Walsh.

Then it became very quiet. Mosely had trained his team of gorillas well. The three subagents—Perry, Tuttle, Plumides—took every cue from the black man, and the first rule was learning how to keep their mouths shut. Surrounded as he was by potentially deadly feds, Walsh was just as content as they to let the silence deepen. He could be quiet for days on end if he had to. He looked out lazily into the street, as if he had all the time in the world. Finally Mosely seemed to understand that the quiet bit had run its course. His voice was almost seductive. "You working on anything having to do with Jonathan Mardukas?"

Walsh frowned. "Who's that? Your cousin's partner?"

"The Duke," Mosely replied curtly, knowing damn well the bounty hunter was lying. But Mosely was a very patient man. In twenty years with the bureau he had run into very few people he couldn't get to, one way or the other. The ones he couldn't get to were usually dead.

"Never heard of him," said Walsh.

"Oh, yeah? I think you have."

Again it was quiet. Tuttle, on Walsh's left, squirmed slightly, as if his balls were pinching. Even the noise from the street was muted by the solid doors of the government car. Walsh glanced from one pair of sunglasses to the next, four identical pairs of expensive aviator shades, peering at him stonily. Walsh assumed a look of equal gravity, then reached into his breast pocket. He drew out his own wire-rimmed shades—the fifteen dollar model, not Porsche like theirs. Walsh slipped them on, taking special care to tuck back the hair displaced by the loop that went over the ear. Then he smiled around at the group with dreamy satisfaction.

Mosely snarled. "Let me tell you something, asshole. I've been working six years trying to bring down Jimmy Serano. Mardukas is my shot. I want to bring him into Federal Court." While he let that sink in, he reached a ham hand to Walsh's face and whipped off the offending shades. "So I don't want to see some third-rate rent-a-thug who couldn't cut it as a cop bring him into L.A. on some bullshit local charge. Do I make myself understood, asshole?"

Walsh hadn't flinched when his glasses were snatched. He appeared to be intently listening throughout the G-man's speech. Now he leaned forward slightly, till his own face was half a foot from Mosely. "Let me ask *you* somethin'. These glasses you guys wear. Would they be government issue, or do you all go to the same store? If I use your name, you think I could get a discount?"

A maddened look flickered across Mosely's face. He nodded to Tuttle, who swung open the rear door and got out. "You can go now," Mosely spat dismissively at Walsh. Then he turned and faced the windshield.

Walsh slipped out of the Plymouth, and Tuttle got back

in. As the car began to pull away from the curb, Walsh called out plaintively, "Hey! You think I could have my glasses back? There's a lot of glare out here."

The driver's window rolled down, and Plumides tossed the shades. Walsh caught them, then watched the Plymouth disappear into traffic. He smiled to himself. Always it was the little things that counted. When the Plymouth had safely turned a corner, Walsh glanced down at the curb. A slim, expensive billfold lay open at his feet. He'd seen it the instant he stepped from the car. He crouched and scooped it up, flipping it open in the proper G-man way.

Inside was a heavily engraved identification card, impossible to forge. The square-jawed black man's picture stared fiercely up at Walsh. The name was printed deep, like a brand on a steerhide: ALONSO MOSELY. Walsh grinned from ear to ear for the third time that day, and there wasn't a woman in sight. He slapped the billfold closed and slid it into his hip pocket. As he sauntered away down Beverly, he looked as cool as a special agent—as if he'd been undercover so long he didn't care if he ever came in from the cold.

The red-eye was starting its descent, banking over the Jersey barrens, with an icy rain barely grudging the first pewter light of day. Walsh had been too wired to sleep, too ready for the chase, and now he sat humming, bent close over the tray table. Carefully he inserted an old black-and-white of himself over Mosely's face on the FBI identification. The photo of Walsh was as fierce and grimly bureaucratic as Mosely's, since Walsh had razored it from his old Chicago police ID.

As he finished the transformation, squinting to see how it looked, he could feel the watchful eyes of the passenger beside him. It was a crew-cut kid, about eight years old, whose mother was curled up asleep beside him. The boy had been gazing, fascinated at Walsh's forgery. Walsh winked at the kid and flashed the badge in the time-honored way. "Mosely," he drawled, "FBI."

The boy gulped and shrank from him, terror in his eyes. Walsh chuckled. "Hey, just kiddin'," he added gently, but the kid didn't look too sure.

The 747 descended through sulfurous clouds and landed hard. The glazed red-eye passengers, pale as the damned in hell, filed off the airliner, flinching automatically at the sight of the New York drizzle outside. Bleary-eyed, they passed the posters for Broadway blockbusters, accompanied at Muzak level by an insipid chorus singing, "I love New York!" Like hypnotized steers, they headed down the long concourse in the direction of baggage claim.

Walsh was feeling the peculiar deep-down griminess of a long flight. He had a scratchy tic in his throat from no sleep and too many Camels. But his mind was speeding on overdrive, and as soon as he saw the first bank of phones he dropped out of the herd. He flipped open his small, beaten address book, flung in a quarter, and punched a number. It took several rings to answer, and Walsh could feel the adrenaline pump with every ring.

"Harold Longman, please," he asked the snippy receptionist, and after another maddening pause he was put through. There were no preliminaries. "Harry," he said, "Jack Walsh. Did ya run the address check on that number?" Having been a cop himself, Walsh knew all about the closely guarded reverse directories. It was a big favor Harry was doing. As Harry began to drone the address, Walsh frantically patted his pockets for a pencil. "Thirty-eight twenty-nine Cabrini Parkway," Walsh repeated, but he still couldn't find a thing to write it down. "Yeah, yeah, I got it. Apartment two-oh-one. You're a prince, Harry. Give my love to Julie. Catch ya later."

All along the cavernous concourse Walsh repeated the

address to himself irritably, still making occasional little pats at his pockets. There was nothing particularly absent-minded about him, except for this one stubborn holdout from adult responsibility. Somewhere there was a pile of a million pencils Jack Walsh had lost. And the only thing that ever scatterbrained him was numbers, so his mind was straining overtime to keep the street and apartment numbers right. He'd had a helluva time back in Chicago learning the metric system, and never could figure why dope dealers couldn't work by ounces and pounds.

As soon as he reached the car rental counter he grabbed a cheap pen on a chain and scribbled the address on his plane ticket stub, relaxing at last. Then he tore through a rental application, fast-talking with the perky blond counter girl. She was a constant smiler, and Walsh could tell she had grown up wearing braces. Any old car would do, he told her, cheapest they had. She bounced off to check the mileage, and he watched her hips sway back and forth in her short skirt as she walked away. Walsh laughed at himself to think what a lech he was becoming all of a sudden. His libido had been in a coma for a long, long time.

"You Jack Walsh?" said a voice behind him, close enough for Walsh to feel the speaker's warm breath on his ear. Invading his space again. He turned around slowly, ending up practically mouth-to-mouth with a man roughly his own height.

"Who wants to know?"

"That's a yes," said Tony Daruvo with a gelid smile. He was somewhere on the overweight side of muscular, and he was a lug, though he tried to wear his business suit as spiffy as Donald Trump. He carried a New York *Post* under his arm, with a bludgeoning death shouting from the headlines. Beside him was a blank-faced young man, bone-thin and snowed with dandruff, who wore his suit like an undertaker. This was Joey Ribuffo, and he had a staring problem. He couldn't take his eyes off Walsh's coat.

"We'd like to have a word with you," Tony continued.

"What about?" asked Walsh cheerfully, full of innocent curiosity.

"It involves big cash and lotsa prizes. Kinda like a game show."

Walsh reached in his pocket to pull out his Zippo, and Joey Ribuffo tensed like a wrestler. Then Walsh slipped out a Camel and lit it. Joey's dim iguana eyes attached themselves to every move Walsh made, no matter how minuscule.

"Let's make it short and sweet," said Tony. "The people I work for are extremely interested in your New York vacation."

Jesus, thought Walsh. *Now* who wanted to kick his butt? "Oh, yeah? And who do you work for, Welcome Wagon? 'Cause I already got all the Tupperware I need."

"An old friend of yours," Tony replied with antic irony. "From the Chicago days."

Unbelievable. So now Serano was back to screw up his life. Had he really thought he could run the Duke down without getting in Serano's way? When would he ever understand that Serano was a death card? It never left the deck. Thrown off balance, Walsh turned and locked eyes with the staring Joey. "How are ya, pal? You always this witty?"

"You're here for the Duke," continued Tony doggedly. "You think he's in New York. We think you're right."

Suddenly Joey piped in. "Hey, where'd you get this coat," he said, reaching out a stubby hand to finger Walsh's raincoat. "Is that a London Fog?"

Walsh bellowed at Tony, "What the hell's he talkin' about?"

"Never mind him, that's just Joey," drawled Tony

Daruvo, making no move to introduce himself. "The way I hear it, you didn't cooperate too good with my boss. Back in Chicago, I mean."

Walsh took a long drag on his Camel. For once he tried to think before he talked, because whatever he said was going to get back to Serano, word for word or worse. Joey's bug-eyed attention shifted to the long stream of smoke that Walsh blew out. "Camels, right?" Joey asked with a tentative smile. "I smoke Kools." The significance of this observation was known to Joey alone. Walsh gave him a poker-faced look, but decided against any reference to morons. If you teased them too much, that's when the razor blades came out of their pockets.

Tony continued patiently. "My boss would pay you a hell of a lot more for the Duke than that putz Moscone."

"How much more?"

"How about a one with six zeroes?"

As Walsh and Tony Daruvo sized up the bid on the table, Walsh could still feel Joey's glassy eyes riveted on him. There was a warm and itchy place at the back of his neck where Joey's eyes seemed to bore through his skin. He turned and hissed at the geek, "Are you gonna propose?"

"Propose?" Joey Ribuffo flushed.

" 'Cause if you ain't, quit fuckin' starin' at me."

The hollow cheeks of Joey's face congealed into a sort of pout. He took a short step to the side, closer to Tony, who bawled at him, "Yeah, Joey, back off for Christ's sake!" But he said it without real irritation. Obviously, he was used to the double-digit IQ of his sidekick, and how he glommed onto people like a rash.

The frisky blond car-rental girl came through the automatic doors from the lot on a breeze of unleaded fumes. She came to the counter and plopped down Walsh's car keys and his contract. "Here are your keys, sir. Just exit through the glass doors." Only Joey gazed in the direction

she pointed. As Walsh scooped up the keys, Tony scribbled a number on the back of a business card, very Donald
Trump. He tucked it into the pocket of Walsh's raincoat.

"Ask for Tony Daruvo," he said. "That's me. They'll
put you through to wherever I am." He turned away and
nudged Joey's shoulder to follow him, but then he had an
afterthought and smiled again at Walsh. "Be good to
yourself, this time," he said precisely, friend to friend, no
pressure at all. And he turned away quick, so Walsh
couldn't answer back anything smart.

Walsh tried to put it all out of his mind as he headed up
the expressway into the belly of Queens. He was trying to
guess himself an exit, combing back over the bail-jumpers
he'd tracked here in the past. Thirty years in Chicago had
given him a real sixth sense for boroughs and outskirts,
and he did better here in New York than he did in L.A.
even. His kind of lower-middle class Irish Catholics still had
a beachhead here, and he knew their shingled houses in his
bones.

He headed off at an exit that was nothing but a beaten
Chevron station, and as he slowed and stopped for a red
light he glanced in his side mirror. Just what he thought: a
dark blue Lincoln had taken the exit right behind him.
Must be Serano's goons, he figured, unless some *third*
party was after him now, besides the goons and the FBI.
Walsh stomped on the accelerator and screeched through
the red light, barely scraping by a lumbering sanitation
truck. The truck turned wide to enter an alley, stalling the
Lincoln for several seconds as Walsh sailed down an
avenue he didn't even know the name of.

In the Lincoln Tony pounded his horn, but he had to
wait till the truck had made the full turn. Joey Ribuffo
looked over, troubled to see Tony so steamed up. Trying to
be helpful, Joey said, "I think he's onto us, Tony." And
Tony Daruvo gave out with a short, hollow laugh as the

Lincoln roared down the avenue. "Figured that out, Joey, did ya?" he said with a certain merriment. "Joey, I swear, you're fuckin' psychic sometimes."

As the Lincoln came to the next boulevard light, there was a huge car dealership straddling one whole block. A vast rectangular sign, "Googie Dorton's Pontiac," rose on a concrete column over "Six Acres—Gotta Move Em Out," with row upon row of brand new cars, gleaming icily in the chill Queens dawn. Tony and Joey craned to look ahead down the boulevard, bolting the red light when the traffic thinned. Tony and Joey were Vegas men. They didn't know Queens from a hole in the ground.

As the Lincoln disappeared in the distance, Walsh's head popped up above the steering wheel. His rented Pontiac was parked neatly parallel to eighty others in the front row of Googie's lot. Now he pulled out, whistling cheerfully, all his jet lag shaken, and headed back to the expressway.

Forty-five minutes later he was parked at the curb on West Eighty-ninth, just off Columbus Avenue, cramming the last of a half-dozen jelly doughnuts into his mouth. On the seat beside him was a small cassette recorder, with a thin wire that trailed over Walsh's lap and out the window of the Pontiac. From there it trailed to the curb and crossed a crack in the sidewalk toward a great belly-front brownstone. The wire ran through an iron picket fence and ended up at a telephone junction box, mounted on the basement wall of the brownstone.

As he licked the jelly off his fingers, Walsh gazed at the generous proportions of the brownstone. A real city building, prosperous and middle-class. He admired it the way he did most things that stood for prouder, more human times. Unlike the half dozen doughnuts, with their stingy dab of red syrup. Hardly enough jelly in the center to taste it, much less spurt and roll down his chin the way he

remembered it as a kid. Was a little raspberry jelly too
much to ask? Born too late again.

A yellow cab rounded the corner from Amsterdam and
pulled to the curb by the brownstone Walsh was staking.
A middle-aged woman got out from the back seat, smooth-
ing the front of her skirt. She wore sensible shoes, and her
hair was steely gray. She reached into the cab to give a
helping hand to an older man, who was shaky on his feet
as he stepped to the curb. The man paid the cabby, and
Walsh strained to see the denomination of the bill, trying
to figure how far they'd come. As they walked carefully
up the steps to the brownstone, the woman giving an arm
to the man, Walsh was startled by how decent they looked,
how far removed from the world where he did his hunting.

As they disappeared into the building, Walsh turned to
the cassette recorder and hit the "record" button. Then he
quickly got out of the car and trotted across the street to a
battered phone booth on the corner. He waited a count of a
hundred, giving the slowly moving couple time to get into
their apartment. Then he dialed the number.

The middle-aged woman answered the phone with infinite gentility, and Walsh said, "Mrs. Nelson?"

"Yes?" she replied pleasantly. "Who's calling?"

"Alonso Mosely, FBI," Walsh announced with brisk
officiousness, loving the roll of it off his tongue. "How
are you this morning?"

Complete silence.

"Let me get right to the point, if I may," Walsh
continued smoothly. "An agent in our Los Angeles office
has brought to my attention a small detail that was somehow overlooked in our initial investigation." Walsh was
winging his rhetoric right out of TV-land. "It seems that
when Jonathan Mardukas was arrested, you were the first
person he called. Now isn't that correct, Mrs. Nelson?"

Still no answer, but Walsh could hear her cup the

phone and murmur to the poor old guy with the shaky legs. Sharpening his voice another notch, Walsh asked if she was still there. Finally the response came, timid and frail. "Yes," she said. Clearly a law-abiding sort. Couldn't tell a lie if she tried.

"Needless to say, Mrs. Nelson, this is a matter of great concern to us. If it wouldn't be too much trouble, I'd like you to come down to Twenty-six Federal Plaza at nine o'clock tomorrow morning. Ask for Agent Mosely. You think you could do that for me?" By the end of his speech, Walsh's voice was all honey and reassurance.

"I suppose so," the lady replied, scared silly.

"Thanks for your cooperation, Mrs. Nelson. You have a good afternoon now."

He could hear the receiver fall limply into the cradle, and he figured she'd need a few seconds just to get her breath back. But he was taking no chances as he exploded into action. He slammed open the folding glass door of the booth with his elbow and sprinted across to the Pontiac. In one clean move, like a soldier diving for a foxhole, he yanked open the car door and slid into the front seat next to the recorder . . .

Just in time to hear the touch-tone beeps as Mrs. Nelson frantically punched a number. After three tentative beeps he heard the line click off, then on again. He had jangled the woman badly, and she wasn't sure, she wasn't sure at all. Again she started to punch a number, this time jittering through six digits before having to start yet a third time. Once more, and she finally succeeded. Walsh cranked up the volume on his Sony and held his breath.

Walsh heard a short partial ring, strangled by someone grabbing the phone off the hook. "Dana?" Mrs. Nelson sounded slack-jawed with fear, her voice hovering upwards to a terrified falsetto. "Dana, the FBI just called. They want to talk to me about Jonathan."

There was a short scrape as somebody else grabbed the phone. A male voice, clenched with control, riveted the mouthpiece. "Helen, what's going on?"

Helen lost what little was left of her self-control. Her words exploded with frightened sobs. "Jonathan, the FBI! They know we spoke the night you were arrested!"

"Hang up the phone, Helen!" screamed Mardukas. "Right now!"

There was an immediate click and then the dial tone. The guy was smart, thought Walsh, just not smart enough. He hit the rewind on the cassette recorder and replayed the touch-tone beeps. Jack Walsh had been born with no musical talent whatsoever, but he *had* been blessed with perfect pitch. It was usually not worth a plug nickel, unless you were planning to conduct a choir. He smiled, flipped on the ignition and gunned the accelerator.

As he sailed downtown to run the numbers by Harry Longman, he was full of the heady intoxication of the chase. If you knew what you were doing in this business, all you needed was a few well-placed friends. Walsh thought of guys like Harry Longman as his very own Baker Street Irregulars, the motley gang of street types who gave Sherlock Holmes key bits of observation. Harry and his trusty reverse directory had led Walsh to the brownstone on West Eighty-ninth and Columbus, and now they would point him to the exact location of the seven beeps of Jonathan Mardukas.

4

WITHIN HALF AN hour Walsh was gunning along a pretty, tree-shaded street in Brooklyn Heights. Across the East River, Manhattan glimmered like a tarnished Xanadu. As Walsh checked the numbers on the bow-front houses, he slowed nearly to a crawl. He glanced again at the address he'd scrawled over the pyramids on his pack of Camels. It was right along here. Then, three or four houses up ahead, he saw a woman rush out through the drizzling rain, lugging an oversized suitcase. The wind gusted her pretty brown hair, and she hunched miserably in the light jacket she wore across her shoulders.

She moved to a new Volvo at the curb and flipped open the trunk. Walsh edged his own car into an open space by a fire hydrant as she hoisted the suitcase into the trunk. Then she trotted back up the walk to the house, cursing the rain in her hair. Her head swiveled furtively up and down the street, but she didn't really know what she was looking for. What did she expect, a phalanx of squad cars, red lights flashing? She was just an accountant's wife. She'd been watching too much television. She climbed three steps and slunk into the house, swinging the door behind her against the rain. But she also left it ajar.

Even as he thrilled to see the half-open door, Walsh's heart went out to all the amateur criminals who didn't know how to play hardball. He pulled the Pontiac forward, close to the Volvo. Automatically he patted the Zippo in his pocket as he got out of the car, taking care not to slam the door. He glanced up and down the street himself, but with a much more practiced eye. He knew exactly what to look for, and was satisfied there was nothing out of the ordinary. He sauntered up the sidewalk toward the house, casual as a mailman.

When he reached the door, he slipped a hand in his jacket and cradled the butt of the .45 in his shoulder holster. He held his breath and listened for several seconds at the crack in the door, about six inches wide. No noise, no sound of voices. With agonizing slowness he pushed the door inward, careful not to squeak a hinge, and slipped into the house.

Even after the gray of the morning rain it was very, very dark. He flattened himself against a wall and waited for his eyes to adjust. All the downstairs drapes and blinds were shut. A diffused sliver of light, probably from under a closed door upstairs, crawled in vague broken lines down a staircase on the far side of the living room. Now he could hear voices upstairs, muffled except for occasional sharp, spitting consonants. The anxiety was palpable. Walsh lifted his right foot and slowly twisted and stretched it in circles to uncrack the bones in his ankle. As a kid he'd been caught sneaking out of his parents' house because of his cracking ankles. Thus he had started perfecting his technique before he reached puberty.

He slipped out the .45 and inched his silent way across the room to the stairs. He wasn't alone, but his senses were so tuned to the murmuring upstairs that his radar was down in the near darkness. A pair of blue-silver eyes watched him from the shadows by the fireplace. As Walsh started up the stairs, the figure in the shadows moved noiselessly forward, no trouble at all with cracking ankles.

With a probing foot Walsh tested the silence of each carpeted step before he gave it his full weight. The shadow followed. On the upstairs landing Walsh could hear the voices more distinctly, though he couldn't make out the words, and there was a certain banging about of suitcases as well. Gliding down the upstairs hall, Walsh stopped at a door and listened. He could feel the sweat of anticipation creep beneath his clothes as he heard a man speak: "Dana, *leave* all that. We don't have time."

Walsh tensed to make his move. At first he felt the sound beside him with his body more than his ears, a low, deep rumble close to his knees, like the first shiver of an earthquake. He spun his head around and stared into the massive face of a black German shepherd, its head hunched between its shoulder blades, ears flattened to its skull. Walsh struggled to swallow an acid lump of fear in his gorge as the shepherd bared its yellow dagger teeth. The low, guttural growl intensified. The hackles on the dog's neck stiffened.

Walsh backed slowly away across the hall. He unclenched his grinding teeth and tried to whisper soothingly, "Good puppy . . . that's a good puppy." But the dog wasn't buying it. Walsh bumped up against a door on the other side of the hall and groped behind him for the doorknob. He could almost see the shepherd's muscles tense as it crouched to spring. Walsh turned the knob and practically fell into the room behind him, whipping the door shut as the monster lunged and exploded against it.

Walsh's knees buckled beneath him, and he sat hard on the tile floor, crashing his shoulder against the toilet bowl. He could hear the dog's sharp claws ripping at the wood of the door, and a sound like a werewolf baying.

The bedroom door was flung wide, and Jonathan Mardukas came tearing out. He looked like an accountant, all right, plain and tidy and manicured, all except for the paranoid look in his eye. "What is it, Heidi?" he demanded of the roaring mastiff. The woman with the rain-whipped hair followed her husband into the hall. "What's happening, Jon?" she whispered, as if nothing was ever right anymore.

Still the animal flung its body against the bathroom door with a savage mix of growls and yelps, insane with thwarted blood fury. Mardukas reached over and turned the door-knob, and the dog exploded in like a battering ram. Now he hurled himself against the glass-enclosed shower stall, behind which a white-faced Walsh braced himself. He held up his FBI badge against the glass with one hand, his .45 with the other.

As Mardukas stood gaping at the trapped figure in the shower, Walsh screamed from behind the glass: "Alonso Mosely, FBI! Get that fuckin' beast outa here!"

Mardukas hesitated. The dog was clawing at the glass now, and Walsh was well aware that all that separated his ass from Heidi's jaws was a sheet of highly compressed sand. As Mardukas seemed about to back away, Walsh shouted again, "Don't move! I'll drop you right through this fuckin' glass!"

Mardukas barked at his wife. "Do what he says. Get her out of here."

The woman stepped forward and grabbed the dog's collar. Walsh could hear the claws scrape all the way across the tiled floor, her front haunches locked in stiff determination. Mardukas swung the bathroom door closed as his wife dragged the dog down the hallway. He put his hands up high over his head and said with a certain graciousness, "You can come out now."

The blood and adrenaline still pumped in his ears as Walsh stepped out of the shower, the .45 pointed at

Mardukas's heart. There was a short, even a shy pause as he got his first good look at the Duke. Bookish and very sober-looking, but with waves of enigma about his eyes. "The Duke, I presume," declared Walsh, more politely than he had intended. Jonathan Mardukas nodded, but without any feel of defeat. Regally, almost.

Walsh cuffed him.

As he led the accountant unceremoniously from the house, discreetly holding the Duke's arm, Walsh was more concerned just then with the wife's hysteria. She stuck to them like a rash all the way down the sidewalk, pleading with her husband, "Jon, what do I do?"

"Don't do anything, sweetheart," he reassured her gently. "I'll be all right."

"Yeah, he'll be fine," Walsh interjected, looking around nervously to see if someone had noticed the scene, but the whole street was empty. They reached the Pontiac, and Walsh opened it fast and pushed Mardukas into the passenger's seat. Then he turned to the wife. He saw for the first time she was gorgeous, yet utterly without vanity. He *knew* this. And she stood there tight and bound up with worry, her limp hair a mess from the drizzle. She was wearing ridiculous sandals that must have left her feet aching from the cold. Walsh said, "Listen, I'll take care of him," then turned away before he said anything worse.

As he went around to the driver's side, he could see her reach out and touch the window by her husband's face. Walsh got in the car quick, started it, and swung into gear, as if the FBI with the real IDs were on his tail. He swung the car in a marvelous U-turn, and out of the corner of his eye he saw the wife put up a hand and wave, but the Duke was staring ahead and didn't see. Walsh tore away down the tree-lined street, icy-gray in the rain.

"Nice watchdog," Walsh said evenly.

"Mm." The Duke nodded. "For five hundred dollars she should have taken your head off."

They continued in silence for a while, Walsh speeding fifty-five in thirty-five zones all the way through Brooklyn, cocky perhaps because of the FBI card in his pocket. He glanced at the Duke's plain face as the accountant stared forward, his forehead furrowed with concern but unlined. Only at the edges of his mouth were the lines of a lifetime of spontaneous smiles. Walsh could feel the force field of the accountant's quiet eyes. If you want to stay in the bounty hunter business you do not get spooked by the eyes of the prey. You do not find anything kindly or decent. This is even worse than feeling sorry, the way Walsh had for poor dim Bouchet. And Bouchet was clearly a breeze compared to Jonathan Mardukas.

The accountant seemed to be thinking, as if he were figuring out his taxes, and Walsh had the impression that he wanted no further chitchat with the man who'd picked him up. But then as they crossed a bridge over aimless freight yards, the Duke smiled and said, "Congratulations."

"For what?" Walsh retorted suspiciously, his guard up against the other man's air of superior irony.

"You just did what no one else could do. You found me." He spoke plainly enough, with what seemed like genuine admiration.

"You got that right." Walsh nodded, keeping his distance. And he gunned the Pontiac and headed up a ramp to the expressway, heading east. The Duke sat silent for a moment, then perked up his head and glanced at an overhead sign, JFK—STAY RIGHT.

"You're taking me to the airport, aren't you," he asked carefully. Walsh didn't answer. It was safer just now if everybody just kept his mouth shut. The Duke began to rub his hands slowly back and forth along his thighs, a gesture of anxiety that irritated Walsh. *Go ahead, mother-*

fucker, he thought, *try something.* But the Duke remained meek and polite, even as he looked around apprehensively. "You don't seem like an FBI agent to me," he said.

"Well," drawled Walsh, pulling out a Camel, "you don't seem much like a duke to me, either."

"If you're an FBI agent," Mardukas persisted, "then why don't you just take me to the FBI office?"

Walsh blew smoke at him. "If you don't be quiet, this is gonna be the worst trip of your fuckin' life."

A shiver of panic clouded the decent eyes, and yet there was resignation in the Duke's voice. "You work for Jimmy Serano, don't you?"

"No, I don't work for that piece of shit." It wasn't so much that he wanted to ease the accountant's mind, but some things simply couldn't go unanswered. Walsh would not permit his name to be coupled with Serano's. "Your bail bondsman hired me to bring you back to L.A."

The Duke nodded thoughtfully. "I've got money, you know," he said, but a bit uncomfortably, as if he didn't know quite how to strike a deal.

"I'm sure you do," Walsh replied coldly.

The Duke shifted in his seat and faced the bounty hunter. His cuffed hands in front of him looked uncomfortably like a man about to pray. "I'll give you whatever you want," he said baldly. Very bad deal-making.

"Start by shuttin' up."

Walsh slowed the car to take the wide right-turn loop toward JFK Departures. He hung back for a moment as an eighteen-wheeler approached from behind and to his left. He tensed slightly as he felt the big truck bearing down to pass him, the huge black tires taller than the Pontiac. He held his eye steady in the side mirror so he could keep his distance. Now he could hear the slap of the mud flaps and the high-pitched singing of rubber on asphalt. And it was at that precise moment that the Duke

yanked open the passenger's door and made a lunge to get
out of the car.

Walsh let out a yowl of rage, reached across and grabbed
Mardukas by the belt, just managing to keep him from
tumbling outside. In the process, he let the Pontiac drift a
hair, and they came within a sickening inch of crumpling
under the semi. The metallic blare of car horns exploded
from all sides, tires screeching. The rumbling bass of the
semi's horn trumpeted the air as the driver swerved to the
left, sending a half dozen cars onto the shoulder of the
road. Everything within fifty feet felt the frozen moment
before a pileup, and then suddenly everyone straightened
out, and it all went down as a near-miss.

But Walsh wasn't counting his blessings. One hand on
the wheel, one eye on the road, he shoved the Duke to the
floor. Then he reached way over and pulled the door shut.
People were driving by him now and hollering at him. He
paid no attention, but pulled the .45 from his shoulder
holster and leveled it at the Duke's neck, the barrel touch-
ing the flesh.

"It is truly in your best interest for you to just fuckin'
relax," declared Walsh with remarkable calm. "Is that
clear, asshole?"

"I'm relaxed," protested the Duke, shaking as he hunched
under the dashboard. "I'm totally relaxed."

The Pontiac pulled up at the loading curb in front of
American Airlines and Walsh slammed the brakes till the
Duke was curled in a ball like a hedgehog. Walsh wasn't
about to take the chance of losing the prisoner between the
rental drop-off and the terminal. His stomach was still
somewhere around his ankles from that last stunt. He
slapped the Duke's head to say it was time to get out, then
went around to the passenger's side and stood at the door
as the accountant gathered himself off the floor and stepped
gingerly onto the pavement. The Duke kept trying to

apologize for endangering Walsh's life; he didn't know what got into his head.

Trying to ignore the effusion, Walsh took a small key from his inside coat pocket and reshuffled the cuffs so he and the Duke were locked together, wrist to wrist. "We're going to be very married for a little while, pal," said Walsh. "But I can't keep you cuffed on a commercial flight, and I gotta check my gun with the luggage." He lugged a seaman's bag from the back seat.

"Mr. Mosely, I'm afraid we've got a problem here—"

"Shut up," growled Walsh, tucking the .45 in the folds of a sweater. "So I'm not going to be able to shoot you, right? But fuck with me once, and I'll break your neck." He gave Mardukas a push towards the automatic doors.

"Mr. Mosely, you don't understand. I can't fly."

"You can't what?" Walsh turned to face him. The Duke's face was grave with a whole new order of seriousness, yet at the same time the eyes were full of ingratiation, as if the man couldn't stand being such a constant bother.

"I'm terribly sorry," observed the Duke with a shake of his head. "But I *really* can't fly."

"Oh, you're gonna have to do better than that, Mardukas."

The Duke wearily shrugged his shoulders. "I don't have to do better than that," he said, "because that's the truth." He didn't say it with hostility, or to argue. But it was clearly the last word on the matter, as far as he was concerned. "Planes are out. I suffer from aziophobia."

"Don't worry, we'll get you a nice big drink . . ."

"Mr. Mosely, this is *clinical*. There's no telling what I might do. I also suffer from acrophobia and claustrophobia. The combination can be lethal."

"Yeah, well, when we get to L.A. you can tell the prison shrink all about it." And with that he gave the Duke a firm push in the middle of his back and propelled him through the automatic doors, even as a parking cop started yelling about the Pontiac in the red zone.

Mardukas died a little death for every person who turned to stare at the handcuffs. Though he tried to stay close to Walsh and hide his wrist, people gaped, and he could see them wondering what he'd done. He was particularly miserable when he saw a tow-headed kid, about six years old, hang back from holding his mother's hand to study the cuffs closely. Then in a loud voice he asked, "Is that a bad guy?" Though his mother quickly grabbed the boy and spirited him away, the kid kept craning his head around to look again, as awestruck as if the Duke were Jesse James.

Walsh stopped at the same long row of blue phone shells where he'd stopped to get the address that had led him to Mardukas. With his uncuffed hand he patted his pocket to look for change, but he came up empty-handed. Now the Duke reached into his own pocket and withdrew an old-fashioned, soft plastic coin holder. He squeezed it in his hand and offered it to Walsh, inviting him to take what he needed.

Walsh jabbed in an L.A. number and waited through a series of beeps and clicks till a weasel's voice answered on Vignes Street. "Jerry, gimme Moscone," Walsh barked curtly, not even bothering to identify himself. The idiot grunted back at him, then put him through to Moscone's office, four feet away through the thin partition. A continent away, Walsh probably wouldn't have heard the click as Jerry hung up the extension. But Jerry didn't hang it up.

Moscone's voice came through the phone with booming false sincerity. "Jackie, baby . . ."

"I got him," Walsh said bluntly.

"Got who?"

"The Duke. He's standing right here." Walsh glanced at Mardukas beside him, who gave the bounty hunter a small, proud smile, as if he and Walsh had done it together somehow. "You wanna say hello, Eddie?" Walsh yanked the Duke by his cuffed hand and shoved the receiver into the accountant's face. "Say hello to your bail bondsman, Eddie Moscone. Best in the business."

"Hello, Mr. Moscone," the Duke said flatly. He just didn't seem to have it in him to be impolite.

Walsh yanked the phone back. Moscone only had to hear enough to know Walsh wasn't bullshitting. "There you go," he crowed quietly. "Jonathan Mardukas in the flesh. I think maybe I'm gonna have him do my income tax on the way out."

"Where are you now?" Moscone asked tensely.

Walsh was annoyed by the question. What the hell did it matter where they were? The last thing Walsh was going to do was reveal the tricks of his trade, how he got from A to B. "I found him in New York," he replied, suitably vague. "We're at JFK."

Three thousand miles away from Walsh and about three hundred yards from Moscone's desk, a rat-gray Chevy van sat parked at a curb on Vignes Street. Camouflaged by its rusty drabness, the van had been parked close by the Moscone office for a day and a half, since about twenty minutes after Walsh had given Mosely and his crew the brush-off in front of Rampart Division. Moscone and Jerry had passed it a dozen different times as they went back and forth from the office, but neither had given the van so much as a second glance. People just didn't stake out Moscone's as a general rule. It was Moscone and his guys who usually did the staking out.

The two plainclothes technicians inside the van saw nothing of the world beyond the blacked-out windows. Their whole specific universe, obsessive and bat-eared, was what funneled to them off Moscone's phone lines. In their high-voltage cave, both men wore earphones, as they sat surrounded by coils of cable and an instrument panel that looked like something in a space shuttle. After a day and a half of eating out of Jack-In-The-Box bags, they finally got what they'd been waiting for. They hunched like bombardiers over their equipment as they heard Walsh's voice drawling to Moscone.

"We're comin' in on American, flight ninety-seven," said Walsh. "We'll be there at eight, your time."

"I love you, Jack, goddamnit!" Moscone responded excitedly. "I really do, man. I'm gonna give you a big kiss!"

"Yeah, save it for your dog, Moscone. See ya later."

And the line clicked dead. One of the technicians held up a scrap of paper for the other to see, where he'd scribbled down "AA/97." The two men grinned with satisfaction, and all the heartburn went away.

Moscone raced out of his cubicle, hilarious with anticipation, and so excited that he didn't notice Jerry quietly hanging up the extension. "Walsh picked up the Duke!" Moscone boomed at Jerry, and he snapped his fingers and made no noise because they were so greasy.

"No kiddin', Eddie. Hey, that's great," retorted Jerry, though his heart didn't seem to be quite in it. In fact, he was so preoccupied he closed his thumb in a drawer. "We should celebrate, huh? You want some doughnuts?" Jerry knew his boss was queer for chocolate-glazed.

"Yeah, yeah," enthused Moscone. "Run down to Winchell's and get a dozen. And get me a few of them apple fritters, too." The man's whole life was a gaudy round of cheap specials and empty calories.

"You got it, Eddie," said Jerry, grabbing his grisly triple-knit jacket and shoving open the derailed sliding door. He left Moscone fairly dancing with merriment and started down Vignes Street at an urgent clip. Humming under his breath, he hotfooted it to the pay phone across from Denny's. As he passed the battered gray van, he took no more notice than he had for the last two days.

In the phone booth, spray-painted in gang Aztec and smelling of stale urine, Jerry folded the door shut and dropped a quarter in. He dug a matchbook out of his pocket—FINISH HIGH SCHOOL NOW—and punched in the phone number written inside. It took four rings to answer, and there was dead silence instead of hello. Jerry didn't seem bothered by the silence at all. "It's Jerry Geisler," he said. "Put me through to Tony Daruvo."

As he waited, Jerry opened and slammed the folding door several times. Like a frustrated twelve-year-old, Jerry was never still. If he wasn't slamming or pounding something, he was jiggling his knee, like an engine about to go haywire. He knew he was big time now, because he had major information for Jimmy Serano's top man.

Tony Daruvo was putting away a sixteen-ounce porterhouse, not talking to Joey Ribuffo across the table, when the hostess called him over to the reservations desk. Tony barreled his way past the salad bar, still chewing on a hunk of steak, but with the air of a surgeon summoned by a call from the hospital. He grabbed the phone from the hostess without acknowledgment. All the steak houses in Brooklyn had been told about taking calls for Tony Daruvo. "Yeah?" he barked into the receiver.

"Tony, this is Jerry Geisler," said the voice from California. Jerry had dialed a Vegas number, and he had no idea he was talking now to New York. "How are ya?"

"I'm eatin'," Tony answered, barely civil. He was still chewing.

Jerry clucked with apologetic regret. "Hey, sorry to bother you, Tony," he said, spilling it fast now, anxious not to irritate the muscle-bound geek, "but Walsh found the Duke. He's bringin' him in tonight on American, flight ninety-seven. They'll be in L.A. about eight."

There was a pause in which Tony Daruvo stopped chewing. At the other end of the line, Jerry was nearly faint with expectation. He'd passed along the vital piece of information to Serano's outfit. He could taste the job that waited like a prize, a Vegas job, big time. He should have stayed cool and said nothing, but the excitement wore him down. He blurted out, "So don't forget me, huh, Tony?"

Tony Daruvo didn't even hear. He hung up the phone fast so he could call Vegas. A big grin settled on his face as he reached for a toothpick.

A pit boss in a black embroidered vest hung up the red phone near the main change cage at the Starlight Casino. Then he moseyed across the pink-swirl carpet, past a long line of jabbering slot machines, past the red velvet drapes to the baccarat rooms, past a fleet of five-dollar blackjack tables. As he approached the high-roll crap table he smoothed the fenders of his black, lacquered hair.

From the back all he could see of the man was his wide anvil neck and the sheen of a two-grand suit. But he could hear him from twenty feet away, shouting exultant profanities, louder than anyone else, generally trying to intimidate the dice to roll his way. And it was probably working. More often than not, the red Lucite dice seemed as scared of Jimmy Serano as anybody else.

The pit boss came around the table to wait for a break in the action. From the front Jimmy Serano looked like an aging matinee idol, but the age hadn't taken the vinegar out of him. He was boisterous and full of easy charm, and only his eyes, which shone blank as silver dollars, gave away the killer hood that crouched in his every gesture like a tiger about to spring.

Most of Serano's bets were at the hard-way line, and still, he kept winning. He hurled the dice down the table, his body thrust as far over the rail as possible. Snake eyes! Serano let out a raucous laugh of pleasure, and three different women around the table who waited on his pleasure smiled and stretched like cats. They were thinking of the furs and bracelets that flowed like manna from Jimmy Serano when the big man was on a winning streak.

At last the pit boss caught the gangster's eye and moved discreetly to his side. Serano pulled himself up from his stoop over the black leather curb and leaned an ear to listen. The pit boss murmured, "Daruvo just called. Your friends are flying into L.A. tonight."

A gummy grin as wide as a derringer spread over Serano's face. He nodded to the croupier that he was done for the present. A large man in a too-tight sports coat started to gather Serano's winnings as the shooter himself adjusted his diamond cuff-linked sleeves—the diamonds big as kidney stones—and strode away from the gaming table. As usual, Jimmy Serano was a man on top of the world.

The L.A. office of the FBI looked just the same as the parent organization in Washington, same bureaucratic numbness, same bloodless chill. The men in blue and gray suits who worked here knew they were holding the line for a civilization that was going straight to hell, but it only made them more purposeful and urgent as they tracked and tailed the scum of the world. Right now Federal Inspector Mosely marched down the main corridor with fierce determination, his three subagents charging along in his wake. Altogether they didn't look as if the line was holding very well.

Or maybe it was just that Jack Walsh was holding it better than they. As the phalanx of agents turned the corner and headed for the elevators, Tuttle cleared his throat and had the temerity to say, "I don't get it. How did he find him so fast?"

Plumides and Perry winced, shot an evil look at their fellow sub, and stared at the back of Mosely's head. Mosely stopped in his tracks for a moment, and his huge hands gripped and flexed silently. But he didn't turn and didn't speak. All he did was pull his dark glasses from the breast pocket of his jacket and put them on. The three other men followed suit. Then they crossed grimly to the elevator bank, where Mosely pounded the call button with a force that would have cracked a brick wall.

5

THE DUKE FALTERED badly as he stepped through the doorway into the first class section of the 747, but Walsh was prodding him firmly from behind and got him past the threshold. A steward purred them nicely to a pair of luxurious seats, and Walsh gripped the accountant firmly by the arm and sat him down on the window side. Then Walsh stretched out happily in his own spacious seat, hands clasped behind his head.

"I could make a habit out of this," he said to no one in particular. He smiled around at the other first-class passengers with an air of benediction. "America," he sighed. "What a country, huh?" And for the moment there wasn't a tinge of irony in it. He was as sweet-tempered as John Denver.

A redheaded flight attendant approached with a couple of menus. "Good evening, gentlemen," she said, tilting her head coyly.

"And good evening to you, dear lady," Walsh replied expansively, taking his menu. As she leaned over to Mardukas, Walsh stared appreciatively at the full swell of her breasts. It pleased him mightily that American didn't require the ladies to be Fonda-thin. Maybe he'd write a letter to the management and praise them for their broad-mindedness.

"Would you gentlemen like something to drink once we're in the air?"

"We'd like your best champagne," Walsh replied with debonair charm. When she passed on to the next row, Walsh turned to the Duke and saw up close for the first time the livid pallor and the darting eyes. The Duke wasn't doing at all well. "I'm going to have a steak," said Walsh, trying to keep the energy up. "How 'bout you, Jonathan? Would you like the lobster instead?"

"I'm not hungry," Mardukas retorted in a somewhat strangled voice.

"Well, then, why don't you get the lobster, anyway. So I can get a little surf-n-turf action goin'." He gave a breezy laugh and nudged the Duke's shoulder. He figured the less he made of the Duke's phobia number the better. There was no question in his mind that it was all hot air. He leaned across the Duke and looked out the window, where he could see the ground crew pulling away on their minicarts.

Within a minute the 747 had swung around and was pulling away from the Jetway. Sweat bathed Mardukas's face, as if he was locked in a hot box. As the plane began to trundle down the runway, picking up speed, Walsh gave the Duke a small, encouraging pat on the arm. "Enjoy the ride, Jonathan," he said. "Hey, listen, this is the fun part, right? It's gonna get pretty shitty once we get there. So take it easy, huh?"

Mardukas started to rock back and forth as he had in the car on the way to the airport, rubbing his palms in long strokes up and down his thighs, as if he was trying to rub away some terrible stain on his hands. "I'm not going to make it," he said in an ashen voice, slowly turning his head from side to side. Walsh was immediately alert and determined to nip this thing in the bud. But just as he started to lay a vise grip on the Duke's arm, the accountant flung off his seat belt and leaped into the aisle, directly in front of the startled stewardess. His pleading hands clutched at the lapels of her jacket.

"I can't go through with this!"

She tried to smile it away. "Sir, you'll have to sit down," she said, singsong-perfect. "We're taxiing."

Walsh could feel the engines kick into a higher drone as he stood to referee the unfolding scene. People were straining to look as Mardukas cried over the roar of the jets, "I will not sit down! This is my *life!*"

The stewardess's smile wilted badly as Walsh took hold of the accountant's arm. "Relax, ma'am," Walsh said firmly. "This man is my prisoner. I'm taking him back to Los Angeles. He's just a little emotional is all."

Mardukas unclenched his death grip on the stewardess's jacket, and she tilted backward a step from the sudden release. Mardukas began to wring his hands, opening his mouth wide and pulling in big, jerky gulps of air. "Now I'm getting claustrophobic," he said. His head swiveled frantically from one sealed hatch to the other. He swallowed hard and stared into Walsh's eyes, the pulses in his temples beating like hummingbirds. He rattled on, running his words together. "See, I've got this recurring nightmare where I feel like I'm losing control . . ."

"You're right, Duke," said Walsh, gripping his prisoner by the shoulders. "You're not in control. *I'm* in control. Now siddown!"

The Duke's eyes flashed to the stewardess, who was trying to inch her way to the crew phone. "How long is this flight?" he demanded.

"We should be in Los Angeles in just over five hours," she said with automatic politeness.

The Duke interrupted with a long, high screech. *"Should!"*

He clamped a hand over his mouth, and spit sprayed through his fingers. *"Should* be in Los Angeles? You mean you're not *sure?!"* The stewardess backed away toward the cockpit, her smile and the tilt of her head locked in place. Two other flight attendants hurried toward them from the other end of the plane.

With sheer brute force, Walsh thrust the hysterical accountant back in his seat, but he hadn't reckoned on the even greater force of the man's panic. A scarlet rash flared on the Duke's forehead as he exploded out of the seat. "I'm in a casket, and they've buried me alive!" he bellowed, pushing Walsh aside. "I can't get out! I can't get out!" He grabbed his chest, struggling to pull air through his constricted throat. "I can't breathe!"

He tore free of Walsh's grasp and threw himself to the floor, dropping to all fours and scrambling like a panicked cat. Walsh lunged and, for the second time that day, caught him by the back of his belt. Mardukas crawled wildly in place, the blue carpet burning his palms and knees. "You can't do it!" he shrieked. "You can't make me fly! I'll go back there with you, but you can't make me fly!"

With a sinking feeling, Walsh could hear the engines whirring down and the ripped sound of the brakes kicking in. The cockpit door swung open, and the captain appeared in full uniform, hat cocked like General Patton. He strolled confidently toward the hubbub, nodding reassuringly to several passengers as he went. "All right, everyone. Just calm down."

Walsh was still half in a crouch as he held the Duke like a collared dog, but he managed to flip out and flap open his badge as the captain glowered over him. "Alonso Mosely, FBI," he growled in his best G-man voice.

The captain looked extremely unimpressed. "You can't

take a prisoner on an airplane if he doesn't want to fly. You should know that.''

"Yeah, yeah, of course," soothed Walsh with a shy, embarrassed grin. "I'm sorry, Captain, I thought he was bluffing. Let's just forget the whole thing."

The captain's jaw quivered with rage, but even he was a little leery of pulling rank on the FBI. The wheels were still on the ground; the jurisdiction was Walsh's, not his. "Look," he said, "ground control is sending a truck to pick you guys up. If *I* was the airline, I'd charge your ass for every gallon of fuel we just wasted. Right now, I suggest you find yourself some other mode of transportation."

The Duke went limp in Walsh's hand when he realized he'd won the battle. As the captain strode back to the cockpit, Walsh closed his eyes and wearily rubbed his temples. He groaned at the trek that lay ahead.

"What the fuck are *you* smiling at?" he snarled at the Duke, loud enough to be heard above the booming echo of the PA system as it rattled off departure times.

The Duke beamed as he bounced along at Walsh's side, eyes lifted as he took in the great cathedral cavern of Grand Central Station. Commuters raced by them in either direction, frantic to make it home. Bums curled up on the benches, and a random bewildered pigeon pecked about the concrete floor, making do without a sky. "I love to travel by train," said the Duke, sighing with satisfaction.

"What do you think this is, the class trip?" asked Walsh, his teeth beginning to grind slightly.

The Duke leaned forward and peered into Walsh's face as they walked, fretting with concern. "Are you always this angry?" he asked gently.

"No, actually I'm much worse most of the time," Walsh replied with antic irony. "In fact, this is a *good* mood. You just wait till I've been cooped up in that little bitty compartment for a while.'' His voice seemed to linger on the claustrophobic possibilities, but Mardukas didn't seem to notice. ''You'll be so sick of me you'll be running for that jail cell.''

''Really? I think we're going to have a lovely trip,'' Mardukas replied, setting Walsh's teeth to grinding again.

The underground platform was a hive of last minute activity. Porters with squeaking carts barreled through, and passengers milled at the doorways, as if to stretch their legs one last time before boarding. The Lake Shore Limited idled at the platform, shooting gusts of steam from its underbelly. In the sentimental haze that wrapped the Duke, it all looked as vital and exciting as it must have been in its heyday. Walsh was more attuned to the homeless wanderers panhandling the crowd, the obscenities written in the grime that covered the aluminum skin of the train.

As the two men approached their car, the Duke asked, ''Are you still going to make your deadline, Jack?'' He sounded genuinely concerned and hopeful that everything would work out.

Walsh was having a hell of a time getting a fix on this screwball. ''Yup, with fourteen hours to spare,'' he replied, then added dryly, ''so maybe we'll have time to take in a nice church supper on the way to County.''

And he shoved the Duke onto the train, but the shove wasn't ugly, it was more like kids playing roughhouse. A black porter with snow white hair greeted them as they entered, checking their names on his passenger list. Walsh was down for compartment seven, Mardukas listed as simply ''guest.'' As the old man led them down the corridor, dignified and courtly, Walsh wondered if the porter had been on this train since the thirties. Maybe the age of black power had passed him by just like the age of jets. The name tag on his gold-piped coat said ''Miles,'' and Walsh tipped him a guilty ten when they reached the compartment. Both Walsh and the Duke were careful to block the porter's view of the cuffs that linked them.

Inside were two bunk beds and scarcely enough room to turn around. The Duke sat down on the bottom bunk, and Walsh unlocked the cuff from his own hand. "You know, Jack," said the Duke with unctuous smoothness, "it really shows me that you're a quality human being for not forcing me to fly against my will."

Walsh had gotten so sick of the Duke calling him Mosely that in a weak moment he'd tossed off his real first name. Already he couldn't stand the grisly intimacy with which the Duke repeated it. He pulled open the door to the tiny bathroom, dragged the Duke to his feet, and cuffed the free cuff to the handicapped railing bolted above the toilet. Then he slammed the bathroom door, sighing with relief at the thin partition of separation. He flung himself down on the bottom bunk and pulled out Camels and Zippo. Oh, shit, was it ever going to be a long trip.

And so, with a lurch and a mighty squeal, the Lake Shore Limited began its gliding journey out of the bowels of the city, headed west toward the pot of gold that had drawn every miner and loony for two hundred years. A hundred thousand bucks was small gold compared to the fabled riches of El Dorado, but it was Walsh's piece of the rock, and deep down he knew he would walk there to get it.

The American docking terminal at LAX wasn't very crowded at eight o'clock on a Tuesday night, the midweek lull having settled in. Flight ninety-seven from Kennedy was the only full plane scheduled to arrive all evening, but even so there were only fifteen or twenty people waiting to pick up passengers. Most of ninety-seven was businessmen who were used to taking care of themselves. Otherwise, there were maybe fifty people in the terminal waiting to leave on other flights, and they sat in little family groups, glazed as if it were the middle of the night.

— So nobody seemed to notice anything unusual about so many men in dark suits wearing dark glasses, stationed around the terminal, arms folded, completely motionless. As the passengers began to pour out of flight ninety-seven, the men in dark glasses grew rabidly intent. They were like stoic jackal sentries, scanning the faces as each emerged through gate twenty, but none of the jackals made a move toward the gate itself. Each of them carried a weapon beneath his folded arms, and once they saw the one they wanted nobody would keep them away.

But the people kept filing out of the gate, and within a few minutes the crowd had thinned to a straggler or two. The last person to come off ninety-seven was a dauntless old woman on a cane, who was swept up by a cheering family and borne away to be pampered. The sentries in dark glasses exchanged puzzled glances with one another. Their shoulders all seemed to droop in unison, as if they had failed somehow.

At that moment Inspector Mosely and his three trusty subs came off the escalator into the docking terminal. With unbelievable suddenness the jackal sentries dropped their posture of readiness. Each assumed the most casual attitude as he strolled past the FBI agents and headed for the down escalator. They looked just as much like hoods and hit men as ever, but the four FBI agents didn't so much as glance at them. It was as if each group accorded the other its proper territory—or perhaps the FBI was just plain stupid.

As they approached gate twenty, Mosely automatically reached for his back pocket, then seemed to remember something that quivered his cheeks with frustration. He gestured angrily at Agent Perry, who took out his own ID and flashed it at an airline clerk with a clipboard, standing beside the check-in counter. The clerk shrank meekly, as if to dodge bullets, and motioned the agents down the accordian-like passageway that led to the aircraft.

At the open hatch, Mosely brushed past two steward-esses who were gathering their flight bags. He barreled up to the cockpit, Tuttle, Perry, and Plumides trailing in his wake like ducklings. The captain was standing in the cockpit door, scribbling a note in his flight log, when the black agent addressed him abruptly. "Inspector Mosely, FBI," he said, never tired of the grandeur of his title.

He was most disconcerted when the captain began to laugh. "Mosely?" the captain mocked. "Are all you guys named Mosely? I guess it's some kinda code, huh?"

Mosely looked bewildered, itching once again to pull out the badge that wasn't there. "What are you talking about?"

"You're here to pick up a prisoner, right?"

Mosely blinked behind his glasses, and his right jaw started to quiver again. "How do *you* know that?"

"He was afraid to fly, so he got off the plane." The captain suddenly looked confused. How come he knew more than the FBI? "He *left* with an Agent Mosely."

A sick awareness seemed to dawn on Mosely, as his hand half reached again to his back pocket. Tuttle gave a small gasp of recognition. With his genius for the obvious, he piped up helpfully, "Sir, that must mean that Walsh has your ID."

Mosely stared at the captain, who looked away in em-barrassment. For a moment the agent was frozen to the spot, as if he could not bear to look around and face the three men who carried his train. He seemed just then like a man who'd lost a good deal more than a card. If you'd taken his glasses off, you would have seen in his eyes a man who had lost his very name.

• • •

The highest point on the Vegas Strip was thirty-two stories, and that's where Jimmy Serano lived, thirty-two stories up. "Top 'o the world," as he liked to call it. It was a line from his favorite Cagney movie, the one where the pug Irishman crows from the summit of a huge oil rig: "Made it, Ma! Top o' the world!" Serano felt more than a little kinship with the other Jimmy, and late at night his eyes would fog sometimes when he'd think how his own mother hadn't lived long enough to see how high up her Jimmy had made it. Hell, an Italian hood could be just as sentimental as an Irish hood.

Right now, as he held the remote telephone to his ear, there was precious little sentiment in Serano. He stood at the floor-to-ceiling window of his Roman Baroque penthouse, all of whose walls were naked glass, without even any curtains, but then they were too high up to throw stones at. Serano didn't like anything blocking his view of the whole of Nevada. With barely restrained rage he seethed into the phone, "What're you tryin' to tell me, Tony?"

From this high up the lights on the Strip below looked as fluid as the tarnished sequins on a showgirl's g-string. A showgirl on her way to becoming a stripper, and then a hooker, till finally she was too used up to do anything anymore but drink and die. These were the girls who never saved anything, never planned for the future, just like Jimmy Serano's mother. She couldn't afford an abortion and couldn't afford to raise him. He did it all on his own. He'd climbed up this far by the skin of his teeth, one floor at a time, and nobody was going to take any of it away from him now. Especially not some spineless pencil pusher.

"I thought you said he was going to be on that plane," Serano said with dangerous calm, his voice a jackhammer muffled in velvet.

Three thousand miles away, his master's voice had Tony Daruvo on a very short leash. The receiver cord on the men's room pay phone at the Blue Blazes bar, Forty-Sixth and Broadway, allowed him to pace only a step and a half in either direction. He had to pee like a son of a bitch, but he'd just have to wait. Trying not to wheedle, trying to sound in charge, Tony replied briskly, ''Yeah, well that's the information we got.''

Tony put his arm out straight and shoved Joey Ribuffo, who was trying to lean in and hear what the big boss was saying. Serano's words came snarling through the phone. ''Listen, Tony. Are you listening good?'' Tony Daruvo nodded. ''I want this mother-fucker's lights put out. So you better start gettin' more personally involved and stop sending other dickheads to do your job. I mean, like, that's why I'm paying you, right? Am I right, Tony?''

''Yeah, you're right, Mr. Serano,'' Tony said meekly, suddenly wanting to push Joey's face in.

''So don't call me with no more stories. Just call me and tell me he's dead.''

''You got it,'' said Tony, but Serano had already hung up in his face. ''Good night, Mr. Serano. I'll be in touch.'' He replaced the receiver and quickly turned to the urinal, avoiding Joey's expectant face. As he unzipped his fly and did his business, he felt no relief at all. He heard the geek behind him draw a breath to speak, and he exploded, ''Just shut up, pal, okay? All you need to know is our ass is in a sling. Now let me fuckin' think, will ya?''

Walsh did his best to block out the sound of the Duke's voice from the other side of the bathroom door. It was the only thing that ruined the delicious, cradling rhythm of the train. In truth, Walsh would rather travel by train than any other way, but he sure as shit wasn't going to admit it to Jonathan Mardukas.

''Jack?'' came the tentative voice through the door. Walsh lay sprawled on the bottom bunk, scribbling figures on a yellow legal pad. Assiduously he ignored the prisoner's call. "Jack, please," said the Duke, a little louder this time, but still with that maddening politeness. "Jack?"

"What the fuck do you want?" Walsh shouted.

He could hear the Duke clear his throat. Then he said, "I believe I told you I was claustrophobic." Walsh returned to his writing, unimpressed. He had had it with all the Duke's phobias, up to his ears. "Jack, I know you're upset with me. Heck, you've got good reason. But it's awfully stuffy in here." Walsh remained stubbornly silent. Whose fault was it that they were here in the first place? "Come on, Jack," coaxed the accountant in the most reasonable tone. "What do you think I'm going to do? Jump off a train going ninety miles an hour?"

If you keep it up much longer, Walsh was thinking, *you won't have to jump.*

With a disgusted sigh he put down his pad and pencil and reached to open the bathroom door. The Duke jumped back and cringed slightly, as if he thought he might get punished. Walsh unlocked the cuffs and led the prisoner out. He lifted the mattress on the lower bunk and hooked the cuff to the outer rim of the bed frame. The Duke sat down quietly, seeming to realize it wasn't a time to chat. Walsh picked up his pad again and plopped himself in the opposite corner of the bunk. Once more, he began his figuring.

Mardukas just couldn't shut up or leave well enough alone. "Thank you, Jack," he said. Silence. After a moment he continued, "What are you doing?"

Walsh could see *that* question coming from a mile away. "Arithmetic," he replied curtly, scrunching down behind his pad to stop any further conversation.

The Duke twisted his hips this way and that, trying to get comfortable with his cuffed hand dangling below the mattress. By the time he had settled his ass, the muscles in

Walsh's jaws were knotted up like a bulldog's. Now the Duke perked up again. "Maybe I can help you. After all, I *am* an accountant."

Walsh was about to blast him again, when suddenly he thought, *Why not?* It was going to be a very long trip. "Well, I was just thinking," he began slowly, even a trifle shyly, "after I turn your butt in and collect my money, I'd kinda like to open a restaurant."

The Duke thought quietly for a moment, as if he was turning to the restaurant file in his head. Then he asked, as casually as he could muster, "How much is it, exactly, that you're getting for me?"

"A hundred grand."

There was an even longer silence now, as if the accountant were suddenly caught up in the minutiae of a tax form. With exquisite care he said, "Does that mean you'd let me go for a hundred thousand?" A note of slim hope had crept into his voice, try though he might to keep it down.

Walsh laid the pencil and pad on the mattress and laced his fingers together across his chest. He stared at the Duke for a long moment. Finally he spoke with tight deliberation. "I never took a payoff . . . in . . . my . . . life." He punched the last three words with an index finger that was aimed directly between the Duke's eyes. "And I'm not going to start now," he concluded bluntly, grabbing up his pad again.

Mardukas studied the bounty hunter—analyzing, judging —then shrugged and relaxed, letting it go. He breezed into an entirely new tack. "A restaurant is a very tricky invest-ment, Jack," he said. As he began to warm to the subject, he sat up a little straighter, not seeming quite so dragged down by the cuff that held him to the bed frame. "More than half of them fail within the first year. The figures are very clear on that. As an accountant, I would have to advise against it.''

Walsh put the pencil behind his ear. He looked at the Duke with renewed interest, eyes narrowed slightly, lines of alertness furrowing his forehead.

''Just what kind of restaurant were you thinking of opening, Jack?''

Walsh had seen every prisoner's trick in the book. He knew how they loved to interview you and get under your skin, establish whatever intimacy they could. Partly, of course, it was genuine need, but mostly they were trying to get close enough to grab the key to the cuffs or hit you over the head. Mardukas was different. He was all caught up in the intricacies of the restaurant question. And he seemed to feel a queer protective bond for Walsh that fascinated the bounty hunter. If it was all bullshit, it was very intricate bullshit.

''A family restaurant,'' he replied, closing the yellow pad.

''Why a family restaurant?'' asked the Duke with a puzzled frown. Walsh looked off into the middle distance, considering the question. ''I would have thought you were going to say fast-food. You like families?''

The question seemed innocent enough, but as Walsh regarded the accountant something passed over the bounty hunter's eyes and closed them off. Slouching further down, he flipped open the pad and drew the pencil from behind his ear. The Duke could feel Walsh receding, folding into himself. ''Not particularly,'' muttered the bounty hunter, not looking up.

He could feel the next question hanging in the air between them and knew damn well the Duke was bound to ask it. *Have you got a family yourself, Jack?* In order to forestall it, he added, ''Kids eat a lot. You don't have to do nothin' fancy, just good food. And families means

you're not servin' hookers and street scum." This disconnected reasoning was clearly intended to finish off the
conversation, and Walsh did not look up again.

But a wave of curiosity and warmth rolled across the
Duke's features. He cocked his head and for several seconds watched Walsh bury himself in the numbers on his
pad. A deep quiet settled over them, accompanied only by
the gentle rocking of the train. The Duke continued to
smile serenely and expansively, and there was no mistak-
ing the air of protectiveness in his face. Fortunately, there
was still a long way to go, because really they'd just
begun.

Moscone glared at the hands of his watch, unsure if
they'd moved at all in the past half hour. He yanked at the
cheap flex band, pulled off the watch, and raised it to his
ear. A blue-green sweatband still girdled his wrist. Yeah,
it was ticking. "How in the hell could he miss that plane?"
he boomed at Jerry across the office. "He called from the
goddamned airport."

Moscone's voice rose in an accusatory whine, as if Jerry
were somehow to blame. Jerry held the early edition of the
paper in his hands, open to "Ann Landers," and he itched
to go back to his reading. Moscone sucked hard on the
long butt of a menthol Doral, then pushed back his squeaky
swivel chair and bent down eye level with the desk top.
With squinty precision he balanced the butt on the filtered
tip next to a row of others, pointed little spikes of filter
and burned gray ash.

"I'm smokin' again," Moscone grumbled, as if the
mute row of butts weren't testimony enough. Then he
raised his voice yet another notch. "Get Dorfler on the
phone," he barked. "See if he's still in Pittsburgh."

Reluctantly, Jerry put aside "Ann Landers"—*how to
get rid of a drop-in neighbor*—and reached for the phone

on the desk. He was very careful not to disturb the little Stonehenge of cigarette butts.

Max Dorfler was curled around a waxy brown bucket of take-out chicken on a thin and sagging motel mattress. The single light in the L-shaped, peeling room came from a battered television whose color had gone to a gray-green and peach blur. The grisly light flickered across the grease that covered Dorfler's mouth and chin. On the television screen, Robin Leach bellowed his soothing promise of "champagne wishes and caviar dreams," as the camera glided over the yacht basin at Monte Carlo.

In the corner a skinny lizard of a guy was handcuffed to an old-fashioned radiator. He was known on Pittsburgh streets as "Dr. Popper," a hippie gone to balding seed, with a ragged skirt of long, dingy hair. The deep-fried smell of the chicken and the sticky sounds of Max eating had begun to make his guts melt—the alternating hunger and nausea he always felt when the smack wore off. The abscess from the street crank speedball he'd pumped into his arm that morning had begun to throb like a hornet's sting. It was going to be an awful night for Dr. Popper, any way you looked at it.

"Could I at least have a french fry?" he ventured meekly.

"I told you no," sneered Dorfler. "Now shut up."

The Bakelite phone beside the bed bleated. Real class joint: phones in the rooms and bedbugs big as frogs. Without taking his eyes from the Riviera beach, Dorfler reached over and picked up the receiver. "Yeah," he said flatly, running his tongue around his greasy lips like a wolf at a fresh kill.

"Max? Hang on a second," came Jerry's voice through the line. Then there was a cacophony as Jerry turned the phone over to Moscone; Della Street he wasn't. Moscone came onto the line with boisterous enthusiasm. "Max, baby," he exclaimed, "I got a job for you! Big money. I gave it to Walsh, but as per usual he's fuckin' up. Whaddaya say?"

Dorfler's lip curled with superiority, like one of the swells at the Monte Carlo casino. "Well, I don't know why you keep hirin' that douchebag."

"Max, you're right," Moscone replied contritely. Dorfler could see the weary shake of his head, the weight of the world on Eddie Moscone's shoulders. Bastard probably made two hundred bills a year, Dorfler thought. "You're the best, Max. You always come through for me. I know you're gonna do a great job."

Dorfler chewed on a chicken wing, watching the TV with an immovable, blank sullenness as he waited for the bullshit to be over. "I'm listenin'," he said.

"You ever hear of the Duke?"

"Nope."

"Jonathan Mardukas. The Duke, they call him. Used to do some work for Jimmy Serano out of Vegas."

"Never heard of him," Dorfler said, still bored and unimpressed, waiting to hear the deal.

"That's okay, Max. It ain't important. Mardukas is strictly a small-time guy." Did Dorfler pick up the change in Eddie Moscone's voice? Almost a thrill of anticipation, as if he might get away with something. But Dorfler wasn't a subtle man, and all he did was chew on his chicken and wait for the payoff. "What's important, Max," Moscone went on urgently, "is you've gotta find the Duke and get him back here right away. Last we heard, Walsh had him collared in New York, but I don't know where the hell he is now. You pick him up, I'll pay you just what I'm payin' Walsh."

"Yeah, what's that?"

"Twenty-five grand," came the answer from L.A., and

suddenly Dorfler perked up considerably. He dropped the chicken wing into the bucket and finally wiped the smear of grease from his face with his sleeve. Dorfler had never been a stickler for clean shirts. "But there's one thing," Moscone added intensely, "you got to get him back by midnight Friday. Or else we all get screwed."

Dorfler's ferret mind was skimming the angles already. Briskly, without a pause, he said, "Don't worry, Eddie. I'll get him."

Back in L.A., Moscone hung up the phone with irrepressible delight and looked at the dull-eyed Jerry. "We're golden," he said, and as he pushed away from the desk, once more he bent over till he was eye level with the row of cigarette butts. He cocked his middle finger against his thumb and popped one butt at a time, sending each one shooting across the room. Jerry chuckled dutifully, but he wished the hell Moscone wouldn't do that, since Jerry was the one who'd have to pick them up. Well, soon enough he'd have himself a Vegas job, he thought, and all the Moscone crap would be miles beneath him.

Meanwhile, as Dorfler hung up in the Motel Six in Pittsburgh, he noticed Dr. Popper eyeballing the television set. With a certain satisfaction, Dorfler gauged that the prisoner would be twitching out of his skin pretty soon. When he dropped the receiver in the cradle with a clatter, Dr. Popper jumped as if yanked up short. Dorfler laughed. "Hey, scumbag," he said with the bizarre camaraderie of the hunter toward his prey.

"You talkin' to me," Popper retorted pugnaciously, with what amounted to his last remaining sliver of bravado.

"No, the guy behind you," Dorfler mocked. He knew he held the junkie's undivided attention as he crossed the fleabag room to the bathroom. From a narrow glass shelf above the sink he swept a tube of denture adhesive and the rest of his prissy medicaments into a brown paper bag.

Almost by reflex he lifted one of the motel towels and stuffed it in the bag—you never knew when you'd need something to sop up blood or stuff in an exhaust pipe. As he came out of the bathroom he grinned over at the strung-out hood. "Today's your lucky day, pal."

"How's that?" asked Dr. Popper, looking at Dorfler with sideways suspicion. Were they finally going to get out of here? And would somebody finally give him some methadone?

Without answering, Dorfler dug a battered address book out of the ratty gym bag he used for luggage. The address book was swollen and sloppy with torn scraps of paper, scribbled-on cocktail napkins, cheap business cards. He leafed through it like a sorcerer looking for the right potion. Then he picked up the phone and dialed an 800 number. He had to wait a minute before he was hooked up with an agent, and he turned and winked at his prisoner as if they were coconspirators. The junkie breathed deeply, trying to calm himself down. Relief was on the way.

"American Express?" said Dorfler into the phone, his voice taking on a worldly air. "My name is Jack Walsh. Excuse me, that's John Wesley Walsh II. I just discovered I've lost my card. I must have left it somewhere. I wonder if you could check and see where I last used it. Here's the number . . ." And he held up the torn corner of a paper place mat and rattled off a set of digits.

As he waited for the clerk to check the computer record, he grinned seductively again at Dr. Popper. Then he crammed the address book back in the gym bag and began to grab his things off the bed and table, stooping to pack them. Dr. Popper, crouched by the radiator, started to rock back and forth like a nervous elephant.

Suddenly Dorfler grew alert, cocking his head and narrowing his eyes as the clerk came back on the line. "What was that? The Amtrak office at Grand Central . . . of

course. And here I am in Pittsburgh already," he added
with a trill of self-deprecating laughter. Now he over-
flowed with genteel courtesy. "Thank you for all your
trouble," he said. "By the way, maybe we better cancel
that card. Don't you think?" From the Cheshire smile on
his face, it was obvious that American Express thought
just the way he did.

As soon as he hung up he pulled on his jacket, checking
the fit of the .45 holster under his arm. Then he grabbed
up his gym duffel and headed for the door.

"Hey, where you going?" asked Dr. Popper in a tone
that was equal parts worry and suspicion.

Max Dorfler snapped his fingers as if he'd forgotten
something. He crossed back to the bed and peered into the
chicken bucket, where two soggy wings lay limp and
congealed. He moved the bucket and carefully set it down
on the frayed carpet about a foot beyond the junkie's
longest possible reach.

"I'll be back in a few minutes, jerkoff," he said. "This
oughta give you somethin' to stretch for. And after you've
finished your supper, you can use it as a piss bucket."

A raucous laugh exploded from deep in Dorfler's belly,
robust and rich with sadism. In truth, his feelings of
revenge were all focused on Jack Walsh, but Dr. Popper
would do to tide him over. He swept from the room and
slammed the door shut behind him. With a terrible sinking
in his stomach, Dr. Popper could hear the pea gravel in the
parking lot crunch under Dorfler's tires. The junkie's nerves
had already started to shred into countless split ends, each
one alive like a bare wire, thrusting out from the core of
his body to the surface of his skin and the stinging air.
Please God, he thought, let Dorfler get him to jail fast,
before he turned into a geyser of puke and convulsions. He
stretched out a hand toward the chicken bucket, then the
toe of one foot, but it was too far away. He would have to

wait till the convulsions had him bouncing around the walls. Then he'd be able to reach his supper, if he still cared what supper meant.

Meanwhile, plump as a pasha in his new Caddie, Dorfler checked the fit of his veal-cutlet toupee in the rearview mirror. As he pulled out of the motel parking lot, he glanced back at the grim motel room where he'd spent the last twenty-four hours. They'd find Dr. Popper soon enough, of course, and then they'd let him go because his bounty hunter had split. And, of course, the scum would be ungrateful. A small cackle of irony percolated up from Dorfler's belly as he gunned the motor and spun his wheels, throwing up a bird shot of gravel. Then he fishtailed at the corner and accelerated giddily toward the Pittsburgh Turnpike.

6

WALSH LOOKED AROUND the dining car, where a dozen people were eating quietly and indifferently, all of them looking terribly defeated by the microwave junk they were putting away. Walsh turned his gaze out the wide night window, where the roll of midwestern hills was buffed by a three-quarter moon. Three or four times a minute they would pass the lights of a village or farm, and Walsh wondered if kids still dreamed of escape when they heard a train whistle in the night. Now Jack Walsh was a rider himself in one of the yellow-lit cars that rocketed across the landscape, bound for the distant places he'd longed for as a kid. Like everything else, the dreaming was better.

As Walsh picked at his fried chicken the Duke sat across from him with several amber-tinted vitamin bottles lined in a row behind his plate. The Duke struggled in his handcuffs to make neat little mounds of pills. The smell of the chicken was bad enough, thought Walsh, without the ripe and overfertile stench that wafted from the vitamin jars. Each mound of vitamins slowly vibrated and danced apart like Mexican jumping beans from the constant jiggle of the train. Frantically the Duke would try to corral the pills, tenting his chained hands, but it was useless. Watching him fuss, Walsh figured he probably drove that gorgeous wife of his out of her frigging mind. What did she see in the guy?

"Jack, this is very difficult," said the Duke, his voice strained from the growing frustration.

"What is this, a methadone clinic?" mocked Walsh, a smart-ass smile playing at the edges of his mouth. The Duke had ordered only tea and dry toast, which waited austerely beyond the circle of vitamin bottles.

"No, these are my vitamins," replied Mardukas, as if he hadn't even heard the drug joke. Methodically now he began to gobble the pills in twos and threes, taking gulps from his glass of water.

"You might as well pour 'em right down the toilet," sneered Walsh. "You piss away ninety percent of it, anyway." He sounded as sure of himself as an expert on Oprah Winfrey.

The Duke sat up very straight and spoke with huffy disdain. "I'm not going to discuss nutrition with a man who eats deep-fried food and smokes cigarettes." Walsh disguised a short involuntary laugh by clearing his throat. This guy was too easy; it was almost no fun. Walsh had noticed in his travels that a certain kind of innocent had no sense of humor at all. Whereas Walsh had laughed at practically everything all his life. "And by the way," the Duke continued imperiously, "people who smoke should take extra C."

As Walsh blinked at him in disbelief, the huffiness evaporated, replaced by what appeared to be genuine concern for Walsh. He spoke more urgently now, his eyes like limpid pools of earnestness. "If you like, Jack," he said, "I could outline a complete program for you."

Jack Walsh had been there before, with prisoner after prisoner. They all wanted to sell you their own particular addiction, or failing that, the antidote. ESP and Jesus and vitamin C, the holy trinity. "I got an idea," Walsh replied sourly. "Why don't you mail it to me from 'D' Block."

The accountant looked wounded, as if he expected better from Jack. "I don't think you're half as mean as you pretend to be, Jack," he admonished. *Wanna bet,* thought Walsh irritably. "Now why do you smoke? You know it's not good for you." He smiled sternly and folded his hands by his vitamins, reminding Walsh of a parochial school nun.

"I never think about it," Walsh said, returning to his puckered, TV-dinner succotash. He had to restrain himself from pushing his dinner aside and reaching for a Camel to blow in the Duke's face.

"Well, that's just living in denial," retorted Mardukas impatiently. "That sounds kind of foolish, coming from a smart man like you." Walsh didn't look up, just scooped the succotash into his mouth. But Mardukas wouldn't quit. "Don't you think that's foolish, Jack?"

"No. Stealing fifteen mill from Jimmy Serano sounds a *whole* lot more foolish to me." Walsh's voice was deadpan. It was neither an invitation to talk about it, nor any sort of put-down. Just a statement of fact.

There was a moment's pause. Then the Duke seemed to change the subject. "Jack, do you have a family?" he asked, taking care to sound casual, seeming to fix his attention on the piles of vitamin pills.

Walsh shot him a sharp look with his ground-zero eyes. He bit off the next sentence tightly, but taking care to leave no ambiguity. "I don't like sharing the intimate details of my life with strangers." Walsh's irony had turned to iron. For the first time since he'd collared the accountant, there wasn't a breath of humor in his voice.

The Duke shrugged his shoulders and spread his palms, constrained though he was by the handcuffs. "How intimate can it get, Jack? Who am I going to tell? I'll be dead in a few days."

"How do you figure that?" asked Walsh, though he knew the answer better than the Duke.

"With what I know about Serano and his business, I'm not gonna last twenty-four hours in jail. You know that."

And though he said it matter-of-factly, with no self-pity whatsoever, Walsh could feel a curl of rage in his gut. Damn it, *he* didn't make the rules. *He* didn't steal the fifteen mill. If you're going to play hardball with the scum of the earth, there were consequences. That part had nothing to do with Walsh, and he was damned if he'd feel any guilt about it. But welling up through the rage was another emotion, a reckless sort of what-the-hell. If the Duke's fate was as sealed as they both knew it was, then there was nothing to be lost in speaking freely. This was a foxhole they were in.

"I got an ex-wife and a daughter," said Walsh. "In Chicago."

The Duke perked up. "Oh, really? Are we going to stop off and see them?"

Walsh ignored the obnoxious "we." He was staring out the window at a railroad junction sailing past—couple of streetlights, barking dog—and for the moment he didn't seem to mind the accountant's pelt of questions. "I haven't seen either of them in nine years," he said quietly.

The Duke regarded him with open amazement. "You haven't seen your wife and daughter in nine years?"

"What is there, an echo in here?" said Walsh, pulling his gaze from the night outside, the irony back in his voice again. Yet still there was something conspiratorial between them, if only for the moment. Walsh was ready to say more, and the Duke knew it.

"This job of yours," said the accountant. "It must have been tough on them."

Walsh shrugged. "I wasn't doin' this then. I was a cop."

"You were a cop in *Chicago?*" The Duke's eyes widened in shock and what could have been delight. "But then you must know all about Jimmy Serano."

"Yeah," the bounty hunter replied vaguely. "I think maybe I met him a couple times."

"Really?" The Duke could hardly contain his excitement now. There was a boyish, prankish giddiness about him that made Walsh think of a kid playing hooky. "What's he like in person?" the Duke added breathlessly, as if they were talking about a movie star.

It hadn't even occurred to Walsh that Serano and the Duke had never met. The poor dumb bastard didn't have a clue what he was up against. For some reason this ticked Walsh off; he could actually feel the skin prickling under his collar. Like a feared patriarch pushed too far, he gave a disgusted grunt and pushed away what was left of the cardboard chicken. "You know somethin', Duke," he said in a low and caustic voice, "you got a way of worming things out of people that I don't like."

He stood up, ramming his chair backward. Mouth clamped shut, he ran his tongue over his teeth, then pulled a fold of money from his pocket. The bill was just under fourteen dollars, and he peeled off three fives and a one, tossing them beside his plate. "Dinner's over," he announced with a sneer, then started for the sleeper car.

"Two dollars?" asked the Duke in disbelief. "Is that all you're going to leave?"

Walsh stopped and turned on his prisoner with a murderous glare. He had known so many frazzled, overworked, varicose-veined waitresses in his time that he usually overtipped like a pimp. He sure as hell didn't need the Duke to teach him about tipping etiquette. "It's fifteen percent," Walsh growled, thrusting out his chin.

"It's twelve percent," Mardukas declared patiently. "I'm an accountant, Jack. I know about these things. Now look at the bill."

All right, all right! Walsh picked up the bill and glowered at it. As he toted the figures in his head, the Duke got up discreetly and stood a few feet away, as if to give the bounty hunter some privacy. Walsh dug around in his jacket for his wallet and dug out another single. *Now* the tip was closer to twenty percent, he thought with a certain superiority as he laid the bill on top of the others. When he turned, there was a look on his face that demanded approval.

But the Duke was gone.

Son of a bitch! Walsh bolted the length of the dining car, nearly sending a waiter careening as he danced to keep a tray aloft. As Walsh yanked open the pneumatic door between cars, a well-dressed woman was herding two kids in for dinner. Walsh stood aside for an agonized moment to let them pass, courteous to a fault. In a buried dead-end pocket of his consciousness he saw the hundred thousand dollars flying away from the windows of the speeding train, like stolen bank loot. There was a sudden hole where his heart had been, but a mobilizing panic impelled and took charge of his body. He threw himself through the door and crossed the no man's land to the next car, bobbing and darting like a basketball player.

As he came bursting into the passenger car, he could just see the Duke at the far end, disappearing through the opposite door. Walsh bounded down the narrow aisle in pursuit, hurtling past a grumpy man who'd just been grazed by the fleeing Duke. Walsh bumped the guy, spinning him around into the arms of a young black woman who was brushing her hair. As Walsh plunged through the far door, he could hear the chorus of invective screeching in his wake.

The next car was dark and practically empty, with various people curled up asleep in their seats, the ones who made do without a compartment and who would arrive in Chicago like the walking dead. Once again the accountant was disappearing through the far door, but he looked around to see where Walsh was. Big mistake: he froze for a precious second as he watched the bounty hunter come hurtling down the aisle at breakneck speed. By the time the Duke slipped through the door, his pursuer was a bare heartbeat behind.

Walsh barreled through the door into the accordian-walled vestibule that bridged the coupling between the cars. The Duke had thrown open the outer door and stood poised at the lip of the darkness, the night wind raging by at ninety miles an hour. The accountant rocked on the balls of his feet, wanting to jump but hesitating. His cuffed hands gripped the top of the doorway. He glanced over his shoulder, knowing Walsh was there, and their eyes locked. The Duke couldn't hide his panic, but he was still more out than in.

''What the fuck are you doin'?'' Walsh screamed over the noise.

The deafening clatter of steel on steel had erased every other sound in the world. Mardukas didn't answer, but he didn't take his eyes off Walsh. The bounty hunter had a sudden flash of empathy. He knew the Duke wanted to get free because he had a life worth running back to. Unlike the rest of the sociopaths and human garbage Walsh had hunted, who didn't give a shit about anything, especially themselves.

With studied nonchalance, Walsh slouched against the door he'd just come through and casually pulled out a Camel and his Zippo. ''You gonna jump off a train going ninety miles an hour?'' he shouted, managing to get the ironic inflection even in a scream. He snorted a laugh and struck the Zippo. Benny Hunnible's lighter that worked every time in the windblown choppers above Khe San didn't falter for a second. With what could only be described as a shit-eating grin, his homage to Benny, Walsh dragged at the cigarette in his mouth and crossed his arms over his chest.

In the freezing doorway the Duke hadn't budged a muscle, though his teeth appeared to be chattering. "Go ahead," bawled Walsh, "I'll get off at the next stop, scoop ya up and mail ya back to L.A." And with that he made an elaborate gesture toward the rushing blackness, as if to say, "Be my guest."

Mardukas stared out at the night and thought it over, methodical as a tax return. Then his hands loosened their grip on the door lintel, and he fell back a step into the vestibule, his body sagging from the release of tension. He seemed too shy to look at Walsh as the bounty hunter strode forward and slammed shut the sliding door.

The sudden relative quiet was deafening. Walsh stepped over to his wayward prisoner and gave him a broad slap on the back. Friendly almost, except a moment later he had grabbed a fistful of the Duke's collar. With a swift kick to the accountant's ass, Walsh propelled him through the door into the next car. All the way back to their sleeper neither man said a word, but Walsh continued to grip the Duke's collar like a wayward dog, as if to punish him by humiliation. The Duke went meekly. He didn't even mention that he'd left all his bottles of vitamins in the dining car.

At the deepest pitch of the night the Cleveland train station was nearly deserted, a no-nonsense depot without vacationers or sleeping vagrants. A strict city police force took care of the latter, and the pleasures of Cleveland itself took care of the former. Everyone was either on his way somewhere already or reluctantly meeting a very late train. The Cleveland station had absolutely no sense of significant interlude. It was used primarily by good, simple midwest folk whose strength lay in fitting in, not like New

York and L.A., where the freaked and the freakish hung out, waiting for the millennium.

Max Dorfler wasn't the Cleveland type.

He waddled hurriedly through the station, gym bag in hand. Every few steps he had to stop and adjust his slipping toupee. He looked like he'd run all the way from Pittsburgh. And just now he was weak with terror, afraid he'd missed the short stop the Lake Shore Limited was making here. He ran down the steps to the boarding platforms and nearly whimpered when he saw the train just a few yards away on Platform Seventeen.

The toupee held precariously askew, he hobble-sprinted to the steps and up into one of the passenger cars. He gulped air into his heaving lungs and leaned against a wall to get his bearings. The car was virtually dark except for the pin lights along the aisle and the occasional pool of light from a reading lamp. Slowly, still gasping, Dorfler made his way down the aisle, peering at every sleeping passenger and trying not to be obvious. But obvious was Max Dorfler's middle name.

As he approached the end of the car, he spied a sleeping head that could have been Walsh, but when he got closer he saw it was a young Marine. He was sleeping in a kind of fetal tuck, cuddling his duffel bag as if it were a favorite hound. In the next car Dorfler crossed paths with the groggy-eyed conductor, who punched the bounty hunter's ticket without even looking at it. As the conductor went on down the aisle in a stupor, every step timed to flow with the rocking of the train, Dorfler pretended to settle himself in a seat.

But as soon as the conductor passed through to the next car, Dorfler hurried forward into the sleeper section. As he went from compartment to compartment, he was irritated that none of the passengers' names were on the doors. Standards were dropping all over the place these days.

Suddenly a voice behind him spoke, earnestly polite. "Trying to find your room, sir?"

Dorfler turned and faced the old black porter, Miles. Immediately Dorfler put on his best used-car manner. "No, actually I'm looking for Jack Walsh's room," he said. "He told me to meet him there. We work for the same company." Dorfler glanced fretfully at his watch. "We gotta get this project done before we hit Chicago."

The dignified porter had learned not to pry into the private affairs of his passengers. Some people ran their compartments as if they had revolving doors. "Number four," he said, "next car." Then gave Dorfler a quick nod, tapped his cap, and moved along.

Dorfler was suddenly tense as an Indian scout as he came into Walsh's car. He dropped his bag to the floor and glided down the corridor, his feet splashed by the light spilling from under several doors. He listened at number four and heard nothing, and no light streamed beneath the door. He squatted to his haunches, his arms spinning like propeller blades to keep from losing his balance. Then he pulled a fistful of rusty lockpicks from his coat pocket. After three precise surgical tries, difficult with the rocking of the train, he felt the tumblers release.

With infinite slowness he turned the doorknob, removing the .45 from his inside pocket with his free hand. It took his eyes a few seconds to make out the figure of Walsh curled in the lower bunk, snoring softly. Dorfler didn't hear the other train approaching till it suddenly roared by in the opposite direction, filling the compartment with splashes of light. Dorfler froze and raised the gun, but Walsh didn't wake. He simply turned on his side and made a low moaning sound in his throat.

The upper bunk was empty. There was only one other place the Duke could be. Dorfler turned to the bathroom door. The blood was pulsing through the arteries in his neck, and his toupee quivered like a mink in heat. He inched open the narrow bathroom door and immediately saw his prey slumped like a bag of bones on the floor, blissfully sleeping with his head on the john. He slept like a man who was either stupid or had nothing to fear.

Dorfler pulled a rag from his jacket pocket, leaned over, and grabbed the scruff of the Duke's neck. The accountant's eyes and mouth popped open at the same time, wide with astonished terror. Dorfler crammed the rag in his mouth before he could even gasp. Then the bounty hunter crouched forward and put his mouth close to the Duke's ear. "One word and you're dead, pal," he rasped.

Still dazed from sleep, the Duke nearly vomited out of fear and the stench of Dorfler's fried-chicken breath. He could feel Dorfler's hands reach under his armpits and start to pull him to his feet. Then out of nowhere Walsh's fist smashed into the side of Dorfler's head, sending him and the Duke sprawling.

Dorfler was up in a flash, roaring like a bull moose. As he and Walsh locked horns, the little compartment exploded with grunts and the thud of smashing knuckles. The two bounty hunters careened around the walls like human pinballs, shaking the whole car. A second later they blasted through the door into the corridor, a single tumbling body of pounding, hammering fists, like a mythological beast bent on violent self-destruction.

As they rolled around growling and spitting, Dorfler's .45 flew out of the heap and skidded several feet down the carpeted corridor. A couple of doors opened, and sleepy passengers peered out, but it only took a moment's glance before they slammed themselves back in again, bolting the doors in terror. Walsh and Dorfler were strangling each other, making horrible rooster screeches, when Miles the porter stepped into the car.

The black man stood there stunned as Walsh tore himself free from his nemesis and lunged for the .45. He scooped it off the floor, swung around, and pointed the barrel in Dorfler's face. Dorfler crouched like a hungry sphinx, but he knew not to make a move. With his free hand Walsh reached into his coat and pulled out his FBI wallet. He flashed it at Miles. "Alonso Mosely, FBI," he said in his most self-important tone, panting though he was. Miles backed away discreetly, ceding the territory to a higher authority than Amtrak.

"How'd you find out where I was?" Walsh barked at the other bounty hunter.

"Fuck you, shit-heel," Dorfler answered sullenly. "I don't have to answer you." And when Walsh yanked him up by the armpit, dragging him to his feet, he added with rabid bitterness, "You ruined my car." Just then he sounded like a school bully who'd finally been clobbered.

He winced as he rubbed a swelling knot on his head, and with a look of abject horror he realized something was missing. His eyes darted in panic up and down the corridor, a flush of humiliation spreading across his cheeks. The Duke, who had stood in the doorway of the compartment watching the knockdown fight between the two bounty hunters, looked down and spotted next to his foot what looked like a drowned rat. He leaned down and picked it up and offered it kindly to Dorfler, who snatched it away and slammed it onto his head like a hat three sizes too small.

"Radio ahead," Walsh barked at the black porter. "I want the local police at the next stop to place this man under arrest."

Thrilled to be included in the drama, Miles turned and opened the door to the porter's closet, where he could call forward to the engineer. But he kept ducking his head out of the closet, not wanting to miss anything. Dorfler laughed contemptuously at Walsh's cops-and-robbers tone. "What the hell are you talking about?'' he demanded indignantly. But before he could say another word, Walsh strode forward and smashed his head into the wall. Dorfler sagged and slid to the floor.

''That's enough out of you,'' growled Walsh, then turned once more to the porter. ''Well, what the hell are you waiting for? I said call the cops!''

Miles scooted into the closet and dialed fast, and when he barked at the engineer he sounded as tough as Walsh. The Duke was looking at Walsh with a kind of awe himself. As Walsh stood over the flattened Dorfler, the .45 swinging easily at his side, he worked his jaw like a lion yawning, to make sure nothing was chipped or bruised. He looked as though all he wanted to do just then was go back to bed.

''Who is this guy?'' the accountant whispered, unconsciously leaning closer to Walsh, as if for protection.

'' 'Nother bounty hunter,'' Walsh replied, bored with the hassle now. He cuffed himself to the Duke, figuring to play it all by the book when they greeted the local constabulary. It was implicit that he trusted Mardukas to play it as straight as he did. ''Count your blessings it's not him who's takin' you in,'' drawled Walsh. ''He's got an abuse problem, see, on account of he's bald. So he usually brings 'em in lookin' like this.'' And he pointed down at the prostrate form on the floor and smiled. And the Duke smiled back.

Most of the Washington Bureau was home in bed, not given to midnight stakeouts unless they were pulling overtime. The graveyard shift sat in front of their humming computers, lost in data. As Agent Perry hustled down the hall to Mosely's office, he seemed to be the only one in the place with anything new to report. He looked as excited as if he had in his hip pocket a list of the whereabouts of the ten most wanted criminals.

He went right in without knocking. The first thing he saw was Mosely's blazing eyes, as the chief agent brooded and glowered behind his desk, hunched like a gargoyle. Tuttle and Plumides sat meekly in chairs on either side of the desk. Mosely addressed Perry in a voice that was dangerously calm. "Good news or bad news?"

Perry reported in a rush. "Mardukas and Walsh are on Amtrak headed for Los Angeles. Apparently, another bounty hunter was arrested after he tried to take Mardukas away."

There was a perceptible surge of power in the room. Mosely's eyes glittered with determination, ready for the chase again. Once more he believed in the force of his superior intelligence and firepower. He almost laughed at the idea of Jack Walsh piddling along on a train. Coolly he said, "I want the jet ready in twenty minutes."

The Lake Shore Limited pounded and screeched into the station at South Bend, Indiana. More than twenty armed policemen lined the platform, high-powered rifles cradled in their arms. Cop cars, marked and unmarked, sprawled across the train yard. As the great bull of an engine ground to a halt in its berth, Mosely and his three subagents hurried up the steps of the first passenger car and poured through the train like a flying wedge.

When they came into Miles's sleeper car, the black porter hoped they were reporters, because he had a lot of story to tell. He hadn't had this much attention since he'd carried luggage for President Truman. He snapped to attention as soon as Mosely flashed his replacement badge. After the drama with Walsh, Miles considered himself an old hand at dealing with the FBI.

"Where's Jack Walsh?" Mosely thundered.

"He got off," replied the porter, nodding crisply. "With the other fella. Two or three stops ago." Miles felt a special pride in dealing with a black agent. He leaned close to Mosely, brother to brother, and added with a conspiratorial whisper, "His real name's Mosely."

"*I'm* Mosely!" screamed the head agent, startling Miles a full step backward.

Next to a long bank of phones in the Greyhound depot in Fremont, Ohio, the Duke stood cuffed to Walsh. They were both looking pretty bedraggled by now. Walsh angrily jabbed a 213 number into one of the phones, as the Duke watched a bum work his way down the whole row, checking the coin returns. The bum wore a long gray coat, and he had two watchbands on either wrist.

The phone rang and rang in Moscone's office, and Walsh waited with wild impatience. As the bum sidled up and reached to check the return on Walsh's phone, Walsh turned and lashed out. "Get the fuck outa here!" he shouted. "Can't you see I'm on the phone?"

The bum skittered away, blinking his eyes. His shoulders slumped as he jammed his hands in his baggy pockets. He seemed at a sudden loss as to what to do next. The Duke caught his eye and gave him a look, as if to say "Don't mind him, he's had a rough day." Then the accountant pulled a bill from his own pocket and covertly slipped it into the bum's hand, making sure Walsh didn't see.

At Moscone's bail office on Vignes Street, Jerry sat crumpled in front of the office television, eating a bag of Fritos as he watched the Three Stooges. The phone on the desk behind his head rang and rang, but he was in the mood to let whoever it was suffer a little. This late at night it could only be some sleazebag drug dealer wanting out of jail, who made more money in an afternoon than Jerry made in a year. Suddenly a voice bawled out from Moscone's inner office behind the partition: "Get it, asshole!"

Jerry was impressed. Moscone could usually sleep through World War III. As Jerry picked up the phone, his boss came staggering in, buttoning up his pants and shaking the sleep from his head. "Eddie Moscone, bondsman," Jerry purred into the phone.

"Jerry, gimme Moscone!" came Walsh's voice, roaring from the pay phone in Ohio.

Jerry snapped to attention, the bag of Fritos spilling to the floor like poker chips. A hundred yards away, in the battered van on Vignes Street, the FBI agents huddled like fighter pilots. "Jesus, Jack, where are you?" Jerry asked excitedly, beaming up at Moscone.

The bondsman streaked back behind the partition to take it in his office. Jerry leaned forward and turned down the sound on the Stooges. This call was as crucial to Jerry's future as it was to Moscone's. And indeed it hadn't occurred to Moscone why Jerry had chosen to stay all night. The bondsman tried to keep from sounding too frayed as he grabbed up the phone. "Jack, where the fuck are you?"

Moscone, Jerry, the FBI goons with the headphones—they all strained to hear Walsh's answer. But the bounty hunter wasn't about to give a geography lesson. He said, "How the hell did Dorfler end up on my ass? Did you put him on this case, you son of a bitch?"

Moscone laughed dryly, too dry to carry to Fremont, Ohio. "Jack, how could I put him on you? I don't even know where the hell you are!" No answer. In the outer office, Jerry strained every cell of his body into the receiver, praying for the location. This was his one big chance with Jimmy Serano. Moscone pretended there wasn't any tension at all crackling the line between him and Walsh. Murderously casual, he asked, "So, Jack, you still got the Duke or what?"

"Yeah, I got him."

All four men on the line heaved a collective sigh of

relief. Once more Moscone lobbed the sixty-four dollar question: "And where did you say you were, Jack?"

"Somewhere between Cleveland and Toledo," Walsh replied with precise evasion. "We're about to get on a bus to L.A."

The two agents in the van locked eyes and bared their teeth in hyena grins. With even this much information they could nail him. But Moscone hollered in disbelief, "A bus?! What the hell are you doing, Jack? You outa your mind?"

In Fremont, Ohio, a woman's voice came over the PA system, announcing the imminent departure of the coast-to-coast. The Duke tugged Walsh's cuffed hand, to make sure he'd heard. "I can't get into it right now, Eddie," retorted Walsh into the phone. "Just wanted to let you know we're on our way." Moscone sputtered, desperate to keep him on the line. "Bus is leavin', Eddie. Talk to you later." And he hung up in the bondsman's ear, smiling with satisfaction at Eddie Moscone's frustration. Oh, yes, it was the little triumphs that counted in life.

Moscone exploded out of the inner office, his eyes bugging out at Jerry. "What the hell is this guy doin'?" Moscone asked in desperation.

Jerry shrugged. "I don't know, Eddie," he said, his feet crunching Fritos as he stepped to the desk to pick up his jacket. "How 'bout I go get some doughnuts or somethin'?"

"What do I look like, a diabetic?" Moscone replied with a peevish whine. "And where the hell is that goddamned Dorfler?"

"I don't know, Eddie," repeated Jerry flatly. Things would be real different, he was thinking, once he was working for Serano instead of this crazy jerk. "I think I'm gonna step outside for some air."

And Eddie Moscone was so preoccupied, so obsessed

with how his whole life hung on a flake like Walsh, that he didn't even stop to think it odd that Jerry was beating it out of there. Jerry slipped out the sliding door and hit the street at a trot, heading for the pay phone on the corner. He passed the battered van as he always did, without the slightest suspicion or recognition. It was hard to say who had the least imagination, Jerry or the FBI agents, who hadn't moved the van in nearly three days. The grease spot underneath it was almost as wide as the van itself.

And at the Greyhound ticket window in Fremont, Ohio, Jack Walsh and the Duke stepped up side by side to buy their tickets. The Duke had discovered ways of walking and standing that managed to effectively obscure the casual observer's view of the cuffs. "How's our schedule doing now, Jack?" the accountant asked with a frown of concern.

Since when had it become "our" schedule, Walsh wondered sourly, but all he said was, "Don't worry, I'll get you there on time."

A ticket clerk with Tammy Bakker hair and batwing eyelashes cleared her throat to get Walsh's attention. She slid the green plastic toward him. "I'm sorry, sir," she said with a certain sympathy, "but this card has been canceled."

"That's impossible," Walsh retorted haughtily. Not that there hadn't been countless times when his credit slate was deadbeat, given the vagaries of his work, but he was paid up in spades these days.

She shook her head. "I double-checked. Sorry, I can't accept it."

The bus was leaving in two minutes flat, no time to play games. Walsh dug into his pockets and pulled out a wrinkled five and two quarters. In his wallet were a ten, six ones and a coupon book for the Santa Palm Car Wash. He turned to the man he was chained to. "How much money you got?" he demanded.

"Quite a lot," said the Duke, permitting himself a satisfied smile. Unceremoniously, Walsh began to go through the accountant's pockets, causing the Duke to blush scarlet. Walsh pulled out a modest fold of bills in a tarnished money clip and flipped through, counting fast. "You call this a lot of money?" he grumbled at his prisoner.

"*I'm* not the one who can't pay his credit cards on time," the Duke replied imperiously.

Walsh gave an audible sigh as he slapped the Duke's money together with his own and shoved it through the window at the startled clerk. She had watched him grope the accountant's pockets as if she were staring straight into Sodom and Gomorrah. "Just made it," Walsh said with a beaming grin. "Two tickets to L.A."

The batwing lashes fluttered with comprehension. Even in Fremont, Ohio, they knew about the stench of perversion and hellfire that clung to the City of the Angels. She wrote up the tickets very fast, fearful of what might happen if these two derelicts had to stay on in Fremont overnight. As she handed the tickets across to Walsh she took elaborate care not to make physical contact with him. The bounty hunter, perverse as always, grinned with delight at her discomfort. Just as he left the window, he raised his cuffed hand—along with the Duke's—and gave her a cheery wave good-bye. Then they turned and ran in tandem for the bus, leaving Tammy to spread word of the most remarkable thing to hit Fremont since the blizzard of '71.

7

SHAKING WITH RAGE, Max Dorfler sat fuming in the holding cell of the drab and low-tech local jail in Elyria, Ohio. He lit a quivering cigarette off the long butt of another. Who did they think he was, anyway? Some piece of scum like the bail jumpers he brought in? Didn't they realize he was one of the good guys, who kept a kind of garbage off the streets that Elyria couldn't even dream of? The two local detectives had ignored all his protests, telling him he'd have to wait, that "somebody" wanted to talk to him. Somebody who?

The worst of it was they'd taken away his toupee. The smart-ass cop who took it said they were afraid he might hang himself with it. Max looked up at the sound of heavy metallic clatter. The detective was leading a group of three men into the holding area, including a brute linebacker of a black man with burning eyes who looked ready to draw and quarter anyone who crossed him.

"Who the fuck are you?" asked Dorfler, addressing the black man directly, never one to cower.

"Mosely. FBI," replied the agent gruffly, flipping open his shiny brand-new badge case.

Dorfler's face went white. "Goddamnit," he said, *"I*

didn't do anything!'' It was getting to be like a bad dream. Irrationally he thought of his precious Caddie, the security and the power of it, and suddenly he wanted to cry.

"Sit down," Mosely replied, clamping a hand on the bounty hunter's shoulder and lowering him to a bench. "I just want to ask you some questions."

Dorfler didn't look very relieved at all. He sat there tightly, his mind racing, as Mosely towered over him. Casually the agent picked up Dorfler's cigarettes and purple Bic lighter from the bench. As he tapped a cigarette out of the pack and lit it, agents Tuttle and Plumides stationed themselves on either side of him like bodyguards. Mosely pocketed the lighter and exhaled a rolling blue cloud above Dorfler's face. He seemed to be making up for lost time in the superiority department.

"Yeah, sure," Dorfler said with eager deference, "help yourself." He was fighting to keep a thin whine of hysteria out of his voice. FBI was very bad news. The baddest.

Mosely looked straight at him and smiled grimly. "Tell me everything you know about Jack Walsh," he said.

And suddenly, Dorfler looked ten years younger.

When things got out of hand, Jimmy Serano could always count on his thirty-second floor wraparound balcony to restore his perspective—only the birds were higher. In his royal purple robe he would take his morning coffee out there, leaving in bed the faceless bimbo of the night before, and he would feel terrific. But not today. As the desert grew more and more distinct in the gathering dawn, the permanently lit signs on the Strip—racing, blinking, turning—gave the sky a gray and soggy look. At the edge of the neon oasis, the skeleton of a new building thrust upward. When it was done it was going to be taller than Jimmy Serano's building. At the back of his mind Serano made a note to find out whose knees to break about this.

From inside he could hear his doorbell peal the first bar of "O Solo Mio." Serano swept his robe about him like a king and headed inside. There was an inflexible rule about not bothering Jimmy Serano till after his eight A.M. massage, but today the rules were bending a little, as if even a king had to get up early to quell a rebellion.

A bodyguard with barbell muscles and a long blond ponytail was moving to answer the door when Serano intercepted him. "I got it," he said. "Get lost." And the bodyguard disappeared without a break in stride, accustomed to being moved about, a soldier waiting to die. Serano punched in a number on a panel beside the door, and the intricate security lock whirred and buzzed like the U.S. Mint. The steel-cased doors yawned open like the jaws of a crocodile.

The dumpy, white-skinned man who entered would have been called Serano's *consigliere* in the old days, but now he was just Sid Lyman. He wore a sharkskin suit with a fresh carnation in the lapel, ready to be buried on a moment's notice. Serano seemed distinctly unimpressed to see him. "Yeah, what?" he said.

"I think you and I should talk, Jimmy," replied Lyman, whose business card said he was a lawyer because the truth was not fit to be printed. "I heard somebody picked up Mardukas in New York."

"You got any more old news, Sid? I'm on it." He padded into the living room and sat on a white satin sofa. Sid Lyman remained standing. Sid Lyman had never sat down in Jimmy Serano's presence.

Lyman spoke carefully. "I don't have to tell you what will happen if he becomes a government witness."

"That won't be the case," Serano said flatly, gazing out the window wall at the offending skeleton on the horizon. He knew Sid Lyman had nearly as much to fear as he did.

"I assumed you were taking that position," Lyman

replied smoothly. ''I'm supposed to advise you against such things. Consider yourself advised.'' And though his neck was seriously short, the lawyer leaned down and took a whiff of his own carnation. They had had this conversation many, many times. There was something almost peaceful about it.

''Hey, Sid,'' Serano grinned, ''why don't you relax and have a drink, huh?'' He lifted his arm and swept the purple sleeve back, flashing his diamond-crusted Rolex. ''It's all gonna be over in just a few minutes.''

Walsh and the Duke sat in the back, cheek by jowl with the bus's thin-walled closet of a toilet. The Duke had asked to sit way back to avoid being stared at. It wasn't Walsh's impression that people stared less on their way to the can—on the contrary—but he was starting to learn it was easier to just give the Duke what he wanted right away. It saved time and trouble.

Walsh tried to punch a little softness into the tiny headrest pillow, squinting his eyes shut and willing himself to a foxhole sleep. Pent-up conversation had been building up in the Duke for twenty-five minutes, spending itself in nervous tics. He bounced and squirmed in the seat like a kid at the opera. In truth, it was driving Walsh nuts, knowing there was a volcano of chatter about to erupt. Poor Walsh didn't look asleep at all; he looked as if he was playing dead.

''You know,'' sighed the accountant, letting it all spill out at last, ''the way you spoke to that homeless man back there in the bus station was a perfect example of misdirected anger.'' Once launched, the Duke was a gassy dirigible that wasn't about to deflate anytime soon. With desperate earnestness, he continued, ''You should learn to focus on what is really hurting you and work on that.''

Walsh thrust an arm out of his sleeve and eyeballed his

Timex, to see how long the Duke had managed to keep his mouth shut. Maddeningly the accountant drummed his fingers on the arm between their seats, as if waiting for Walsh to give a proper account of himself. When Walsh remained silent, the interrogation escalated. The Duke said, "Can I ask you why you haven't seen your wife and daughter in nine years?"

Would it matter if Walsh said no? Sooner or later the Duke was going to worm it out of him, anyway. "My ex got married to a police captain," replied the bounty hunter tonelessly. "I'm not exactly popular with the Chicago Police Department."

The Duke was utterly still for a moment. Walsh had a pang of hope that maybe he'd given the accountant enough to chew on for a while. No such luck. "Did you do something wrong?" asked the Duke, almost shyly, like a kid who wanted to trade a dirty secret.

An involuntary twinge passed across Walsh's face, rather as if he were having a root canal. "Yeah, I guess so," he said with tight irony. "I tried to bust this big-time dealer. Guy practically supplied the whole city with H. I got real close to him, gained his confidence. Took me over a year." Walsh was speaking just now as precisely as if he were giving testimony. It also sounded as though he hadn't said any of it in a long, long time. "But then, just when I was ready to nail the son of a bitch," and he stretched out the next word with broad sarcasm, *"mysteriously,* my fellow officers discovered seven pounds of heroin in my bedroom closet."

Beside him the Duke let out a low, sympathetic whistle. Walsh seemed to take it as a vote of confidence, and he warmed up considerably as he spoke the climax to his tale. "They gave me a choice," he said, ticking them off on his fingers. "Get on the payroll like everyone else. Get out of town. Thirty years in the federal pen."

The accountant nodded and spoke right away. "So I guess any offer I might make would be a waste of time." Walsh's silence was all the answer he needed. "Let me ask you something," he went on—and Walsh grunted, wishing the Duke would stop asking if he could ask everything, since he always asked it anyway—"do you miss your wife and daughter?"

"I don't think about it much," Walsh replied quietly.

The Duke's tongue made a clucking sound. "There's that denial thing again, Jack. We're going to be going through Chicago in a couple of hours." His hand touched Walsh's arm on the armrest, just short of an affectionate squeeze. "I think it would be good for you to look them up."

As if Walsh had not already thought it. The bounty hunter swallowed a curl of bile, furious to think the Duke would try to finagle him into it. Yet he sounded curiously mild when at last he answered, rather as if he were talking to a friend—if he'd ever had such a thing, that is. "I know in some twisted way you mean well," he said, "but will you please stay out of my personal life?"

But the Duke could not leave it without one more foray into pop psychology. Expecting no answer at all, earnest as Ann Landers, he declared, "You can't just avoid the things that hurt you, Jack. You've got to attack them head on. Sooner or later, you know, you're going to have to take a front-row approach to life. Or else, what's the point?"

Of course, he didn't answer. Finally the Duke had come to the end of the latest interrogation, and he turned away to the window to signal that Jack could go back to sleep again. But Jack was wide awake now. He stared down the aisle of the bus and scarcely blinked his eyes. He would have been a lot safer if he'd yelled at the Duke as usual and told him to button his lip.

• • •

In the holding cell in Elyria, a blue-suited man in dark glasses had joined the three other FBI agents. He was huddled with Mosely in the corner, and no matter how Dorfler perked his ears to listen he couldn't make out what they were saying.

"Walsh called Moscone about a half hour ago," Agent Perry murmured to his boss. "From outside of Toledo. He's on a Greyhound headed for Chicago."

"Let's go," Mosely barked to the others. The driven look was in his eyes again.

His three subagents fell into step behind him, and the local sergeant suddenly seemed bewildered. "Wait," he called after Mosely, "what do we do with this guy?"

"Let him go," came the answer, totally indifferent, as the pack of agents swept out into the higher world of blood pursuit.

Max Dorfler, rising from the bench with a scrap of his dignity intact, would not even deign to look at the sergeant as he grabbed up his coat. He slapped at the pockets irritably, but of course Mosely had palmed his cigarettes as well as his lighter. Suddenly the sergeant reached out and offered him a Winston Light. Dorfler took it with a sniff of disdain and let the sergeant light it for him. They stood there together for a moment like two small survivors whom all the glory has long passed by.

The Greyhound station in Gary, Indiana was the sleepiest place in the world. Nothing had ever happened there, and nothing was in the planning stage. Yet from where Tony Daruvo sat in the big black Chrysler in the parking lot, there seemed to be a killer everywhere he looked. Tony knew most of them pretty well, but a few were local talent contracted out for this job only, from Cleveland or Cincinnati.

He couldn't quite place the slender man next to the bank of soft drink machines, but he had a good idea what was in the long gold box under the man's arm. It wasn't a dozen roses. Another new guy in the terminal, dressed in janitor's overalls, never took his right hand out of his baggy pocket. Tony knew all the men at the entrances and exits, though not by name. Everybody was named Big Eddie, more or less. The guy that Tony *really* respected was on the roof of the warehouse across the street with an M-16 and a long-range sight. He never missed.

Beside Tony in the Chrysler was Joey Ribuffo, wired as ever. For an hour now, not a minute had passed without Joey jittering his knee up and down like an idling motor. For the tenth time he reached up and flicked the silver-sequined stripper's tassel that hung from the rearview mirror. Not able to take it for one more second, Tony grabbed the tassel and tore it off the mirror.

"What's wrong with you?" Tony nearly shouted. Joey looked at him, open-mouthed and uncomprehending. "Do you have to *touch* everything? That's very fuckin' annoying."

Joey blinked respectfully and glanced out the window. With the hit men scattered around, the station looked like a chessboard, almost checked. Joey said, "Do you think we'll get 'em?"

"Fuck. They can't *all* miss," retorted Tony dryly. But the way things had been going lately, he sounded a whole lot surer than he felt.

The 5:17 for Chicago swung from the street into the parking lot, belching black exhaust and squealing to a stop in the first bay by the terminal entrance. The door folded open with a pneumatic hiss, and the bedraggled passengers stepped down one at a time. Each one paused on the pavement, glancing around for the snack bar or a *real* bathroom. Meanwhile, the man by the Coke machine stooped to open the flower box. A guy at the magazine stand closed his copy of *Boxing*. The sniper on the warehouse roof lifted the rifle to his shoulder and focused the cross hairs on the bus door.

Inside the bus, Walsh stood up in the aisle and ordered the Duke to follow suit. Walsh arched his back and stretched his arms and yawned. The Duke's right arm, still connected by the umbilical handcuffs, flapped in the air like a marionette's. He looked out the window with a wistful stare. "Can't I stretch my legs a little?" he asked.

"Sure, if you can do it right here. I don't want to attract no attention."

The accountant's face scrunched up in a fretful whine. "C'mon, Jack, we're going to be stuck on this thing for two days. Please . . . my claustrophobia."

Walsh straightened up and considered a moment, wistful, in fact, for a little fresh air himself. He peered at the Duke suspiciously, then relented. "Okay, Duke. But if you pull any more shit with me, you'll be in the market for prosthetic kneecaps."

He started down the aisle to the front of the bus, dragging his prisoner behind him. As they reached the door, a short and dumpy Asian woman stepped out of the sniper's cross hairs. For a moment the death space was empty. Walsh clumped down the steps of the bus, the Duke a measured step behind.

In the hair-trigger second that followed, the bus station exploded into sudden, violent life: racing engines, men running, car doors slamming, spinning red and blue lights. Out of nowhere a fleet of tan and gray federal cars came fishtailing into the lot, slamming their brakes as they circled the bus. Two men sprang from each car and hunched behind the open doors, their guns steady on the furrowed spot between Walsh's eyes. Mosely's car was the last one in, like a skidding, screeching exclamation point to the whole fluid operation. The black agent threw open his door and led his three trusty subagents to the bus in long, pounding strides.

In the Chrysler, Tony's and Joey's jaws fell open at the same moment, though Joey's didn't have far to fall. "Who the hell are *those* guys?" asked Tony Daruvo in offended disbelief.

"They with us?" wondered the dimwit Joey, but for once he had a point.

"Oh, jeez, it's the fuckin' feds," acknowledged Tony with a sinking heart.

Before Walsh or the Duke had time to formulate even that much of an answer, Agent Perry grabbed the bounty hunter by the shoulder and spun him around, mashing his face into the side of the mud-streaked Greyhound. Instinctively, the Duke started to reach for Perry to pull him off Walsh, but before he could move Tuttle and Plumides had smashed him into the bus as well, his cheek and lips flattened like clay. Meanwhile more Feds and local cops swarmed around the bus like a pep rally. Methodically Tuttle kicked open the Duke's legs into a painfully wide spread eagle, as Perry did the same to Walsh.

Then Perry leaned close to Walsh's ear and whispered through clenched teeth, "One move and I'll spray your brains all over this bus."

The voices of the cops near Walsh and the Duke quieted down, as they shuffled apart and left a broad path for Mosely to saunter through. The black agent motioned for Tuttle to step aside from the Duke, who now raised his face from the bus and squinted into Mosely's dead-on stare. "You and I have a lot of talking to do," said Mosely, as if he had all the time in the world now. Then he slipped his aviator glasses on and jutted his chin toward Walsh. He gestured to Perry to release the back of Walsh's neck. "Remember me?" he asked with a smile.

"Oh, yeah," said Walsh, rubbing the grease from his

cheek. "Agent Foster Grant." Then he brightened. "Hey, Alonso, aren't ya gonna thank me for doing your job so good?"

Mosely's smile stiffened, so slightly that only Walsh noticed, but enough for Mosely to realize he'd broken his own cardinal rule: Never let anyone know they've gotten to you. Ever. "Thanks, Walsh," he said with as much irony as he could muster, and just then, across the street, the sniper leveled his M-16 at the Duke's forehead and squeezed the trigger.

Something hot stung the air beside the accountant's ear. At the same instant a nickel-sized hole appeared in the aluminum siding of the bus, half an inch from his head. He never understood afterwards how come everyone else reacted so much quicker than he, but then he must have been slightly in shock, because he didn't even hear the sound of the gunshot. He saw Mosely swing the .38 out of his holster and all the other agents jump as the sniper fired again. A local cop, not much higher than traffic, took it in the shoulder and spun to the pavement.

Everything then erupted into screams and running feet, as Walsh tackled the Duke and they both crashed to the ground. The hit man with the gold-boxed Uzi fired in a sweep, and four of the bus's windows popped, spraying shattered heaps of bottle-green crystals. The gang of local hoods inside the terminal stood in a staggered row near the main double doors of the station, looking like a nightmare firing squad. Everyone with a gun seemed to need to shoot it now, even if nobody knew anymore exactly what the target was.

On the pavement beside the bus, with Walsh's body covering him, Mardukas breathed the acrid smell of gunpowder into his heaving lungs. From underneath Walsh, in the tiny wedge of what remained of his view, he saw a woman's green high-heeled shoe tipped over on its side.

Cascading explosions of gunfire, zinging ricochets off the pavement pounded against his eardrums. The man at the magazine rack fired off a burst from his machine pistol and drilled the asphalt by the Duke's head, stinging his eyes with gravel.

Perry spun around and dropped the guy, who dragged the magazine rack over with him, spilling an avalanche of junk news. Mosely crouched beside Walsh and the Duke, aiming dead-on at the sniper on the roof. "Freeze!" he bellowed, his voice deep and resonant as a church organ. The sniper pivoted on one knee to fire. But before he could get his cross hairs matched, Mosely blew him away with a shot to the belly, doubling him up, blasting him off the roof. Exultant, Mosely sprinted around to the back of the bus to cover Tuttle and Plumides. All the agents had managed to lose their beloved dark glasses.

Stunned and scrunched down in his seat in the black Chrysler, Tony Daruvo twisted the ignition key and yelped at Joey Ribuffo, "Fuck this!"

Joey, of course, was too stupid to duck, and he watched the cacophonous gunplay as though he was sitting at a drive-in movie. "Yeah, hit it!" he shouted back at Tony, though he would have gladly had them plow right into the station. Joey liked noise. He hooted and banged the armrest as Tony, still ducking down like a man without a neck, floored the Chrysler and rocketed out of the parking lot.

As the Chrysler passed the bus in a whoosh of exhaust, Walsh got off the Duke and dragged him up to his knees. He pointed across at the nearest car, the unmarked tan FBI four-door that Mosely and his men had jumped out of. The two front doors gaped open. Walsh and the Duke scooted for it in a running crouch and tumbled into the front seat, trying not to strangle each other on the cuffs that bound them together.

Government-issue keys dangled from the ignition. Walsh pushed the Duke to the passenger's side and bawled at him to close the door. As the bounty hunter turned the key, the engine gunned to life. Walsh stomped the accelerator and sped for the exit in a squealing fishtail. As he took the dip out of the driveway at forty, he and the Duke bounced in unison and smacked their heads on the roof.

They veered away down the street, and Walsh felt a bad vibration in the seat beneath him. He'd warped the alignment good, he figured, then suddenly realized it was the Duke, whose body trembled beside him with deathly fear. He shook like a man who couldn't get warm. There was an elemental force about him, his eyes like saucers, his breath coming fast in tight rolling waves. His words when they came were disjointed, pitched to a terror all their own, unable to keep up with the reels playing and playing in his head. He kept seeing that green high-heeled shoe.

"Oh, God! Oh, my God! Let me go," he caterwauled, one hand scraping the door handle.

Walsh gave him a solid uppercut to the chest with his elbow, knocking him back in his seat. "Shut up! Just shut the fuck up!"

"What *was* that?" pleaded the accountant. "Why would they shoot at us like that?"

"Serano's people," Walsh barked. "He's not even waiting until you get to jail."

The Duke made several tries with his quaking hands before he could steady himself enough to pick up a clipboard that had fallen to the floor under the dash. He stared at the printing on a memo. "Alonso Mosely?" he read in disbelief. "Isn't that the name *you've* been using?"

"Gimme that," growled the bounty hunter, snatching the clipboard. Oh, it *would* be, wouldn't it, Walsh thought grimly, scanning the memo beneath the agent's name. Somehow Jack Walsh would end up with Mosely's car.

Fate had collared the two of them in some twisted joke. "Well, isn't that nice," Walsh said with icy irony. "I guess I better make sure I keep it gassed up for him."

A shadow of distrust passed over the Duke's strained face. "But wait," he said, "if you want to turn me in, why are you running away from the FBI?"

" 'Cause I only get my money if I deliver you to L.A., not to the feds." Then something on the clipboard made Walsh slap his forehead and drop his jaw. "Goddamnit! They got a tap on Moscone's phone!" No wonder everyone always knew where he was.

As they came over the rise of a low hill, a black-and-white helicopter came roaring toward them across the sky. Walsh felt a chill ripple down from the top of his head, like the feeling an instant before you get busted. His heart suspended as the chopper whipped the air above their heads, but apparently it was hell-bent for the bus station. Its steady, staccato panting faded as it sailed off. Walsh and the Duke let loose a collective sigh.

Walsh turned and stared at the accountant, who was calmer now. Since when had it become "us" and "them?" For a reason Walsh didn't entirely understand, the Duke was on his side. The bounty hunter pulled off the main road and nosed the car in among some trees and killed the motor. "We're not going to get too far in a stolen FBI car," he said, and the Duke nodded judiciously, rather like a copilot.

When they climbed out of Mosely's car, Walsh reached into his jacket and pulled out his dark glasses. With great deliberation he misted them with his breath and buffed them on his sleeve, then carefully set them on the steering wheel.

"What's that for?" asked the Duke.

"Inside joke," replied Walsh with a grin, "between me and my pal Alonso."

• • •

"What was that again?" asked Jimmy Serano softly into the phone. His eyes were absolutely still, and the rest of his face pulled back from his feral teeth like a dog's snarling muzzle.

"I'm real sorry, Mr. Serano," Tony Daruvo pleaded, trying not to whine. But fear and the telephone speaker-box gave his voice a thin and mewling sound. "It didn't happen. Too much confusion." Serano didn't answer, but what he was thinking was, *You don't know sorry*. Tony blundered on. "There was about thirty feds there, plus a buncha local heat. A lotta heads got popped."

Sid Lyman slumped at the bar in Serano's penthouse, anxiously watching his client as Serano stood grimly holding the phone. Sid groaned and rubbed his eyes, then suddenly clenched his fists with an awful thought. He swung off the barstool and crossed to Serano. "Hey, Jimmy, you better get off the line . . ."

"Shut up," said Serano, quick and soft, as if he were flicking away a fly.

"Look, if they got a tap—"

"I said shut up!" exploded Serano. The seismic rumble of his rage snapped Sid's head back. And fifteen hundred miles away in Ohio, Tony Daruvo's face contorted as if some part of his body were being likewise twisted. He stood next to Joey Ribuffo at a pay phone in a mini-mart, while the retard polished off a box of Cracker Jacks. When Serano screamed even Joey could hear it, and he slunk a step away from Tony as he tapped the bottom of the box to get the crumbs.

"Where's Mardukas? In custody?" Serano was quiet again, but his jaw muscles rolled in knots, and the vein running like a gash down the middle of his forehead was swollen and blue.

"I don't know," replied Tony Daruvo with a wince,

and Serano said nothing. Tony liked it better when he was hollering. "There was so much commotion, see. I don't know where the fuck he is."

At that moment Joey Ribuffo fished out his prize from the bottom of the box. It was a little red whistle, the shape of a bird. Tentatively Joey began to blow it. He liked what he heard and blew louder. Tony, who was batshit from the silence at the other end of the phone, turned and grabbed a handful of Joey's collar. "Will you just back the fuck off?" he screamed.

Serano's voice snapped Tony to attention. "Let me make it real simple for you guys," he said, mild as a glassy sea above a school of barracuda. "I am not to get another phone call like this." Even as Tony nodded, the phone clicked in his ear. He felt an ache deep in his throat and nearly wept with relief, to think he had another chance.

And in Vegas, Jimmy Serano swung his arm like a baseball bat at the speaker-phone. It smashed against the wall with a beige explosion of plastic shards. "I should've killed that son of a bitch Walsh back in Chicago," he growled, as poor Sid Lyman hunkered ever deeper into his shoulders, till he looked like a wounded turtle.

8

"I CAN'T BELIEVE this," said Walsh, shaking his head, bewildered. "I haven't seen them in nine years, and the first thing outa my mouth is gonna be 'Can I borrow a few hundred bucks?'"

And with that he handed his last seven bills, all singles, to the cabby, who lurched away and left the two men standing on the curb staring at her house. It was worse than he'd expected, thought Walsh. It was beautiful. A lot of cop's days off had been spent mowing, feeding, watering, rolling that swath of suburban lawn. It was a deep Irish green, even among the compulsively manicured yards that lined the middle-class street. Walsh knew that cops spent a lot of time on their homes because a proper house was the dividing line between "this is mine" and "the scum out there." He and Gail had had a much smaller place than this, but he'd kept it as nice.

"I have a feeling this is going to be very good for you," said the Duke.

They walked up the S-shaped concrete path, and Walsh appeared transfixed by every contour. With the cuffs they'd learned to walk together in a kind of unison without the accountant having to do a little hop every couple of steps.

The Duke couldn't help but think of the early days with his own wife—his only girl, his only reason. He could stand anything, even this whole Serano nightmare, as long as he had her. With an ache of fellow feeling, he reached across with his free hand and patted Walsh's shoulder.

The bounty hunter made a feeble attempt to brush his shaggy hair with his fingers. The Duke tugged the cuffs and brought them to a stop at the bottom of the steps that led to the front door. Making a critical, straight-on examination, the Duke straightened Walsh's collar and brushed at the wrinkles in his jacket. For once Walsh didn't complain about being smothered, and he even let the Duke fix the part in his hair. He looked horribly vulnerable all of a sudden, as if he needed some kind of essential approval before going forward.

"You look great," the Duke assured him, sounding almost as if he meant it.

They climbed the brick steps to the door. Walsh reached over and pressed the bell. As they waited expectantly they could hear from inside a shouted voice, then the muffled sound of feet on the carpeted stairs, fast and running like a child's. The door was opened by a boy of about seven, with light brown hair and an instantly suspicious expression. "Who are you guys?" he asked, tough like a cop's kid.

"I'm your mother's ex-husband," Walsh replied with utter control and politeness.

The door slammed in his face. Walsh and the Duke stood facing ahead, neither of them quite sure what to say. They could hear the kid call "Mom," loud but without any urgency. Just to break the silence the accountant said, "Nice boy," but it was so obviously a load of bull that both men started to snicker. It might even have grown to a full-belly laugh, shared by the men as if they were comrades rather than two men cuffed at the wrist. Except suddenly the door opened again, and there was Gail.

Walsh's laughter stopped on a dime, leaving the shape of a smile on his face and stunned eyes. She was still the only woman he'd ever seen with a natural redness in her cheeks, like a constant sunburn in that one place only. She was wearing her ash-blond hair long now, even longer than when they'd first met. It was tied loosely in back, but had fallen partially out of the knot and billowed down in a wide arc, almost to her shoulders.

"Jack," she said.

Walsh felt a stinging pressure behind his eyes, and a pulsing emptiness somewhere in his gut. Like being slammed very hard. He'd almost gotten used to the memory of her, like a good luck charm in a secret place. Now she was so fresh and new, he felt as raw as the first night he ever had to spend without her. The voice was exactly the same. He used to tell her it sounded as if it had been rubbed with a fine-grain sandpaper, then dipped in honey. Especially when she laughed.

"Hi, Gail," Walsh replied, as easy as she, but then he didn't know what to say, and neither did she. Their eyes stayed fixed on each other, and the Duke could feel the strain of it, as if the air were heavy with woodsmoke. Finally the accountant cleared his throat, and the sound dissolved the spell a bit, allowing Gail to speak.

"They mentioned you and him on the news this morning. Are you all right?"

He nodded. She laughed shyly, a single dry, unreal laugh. She looked down, but Walsh's eyes never left her face for an instant. It looked to the Duke as if he was trying to memorize her. When Walsh at last spoke, he seemed to have given up trying to hide the desperation in his voice. "Can I come in for a minute?"

She nodded and stepped back into the foyer, opening the

door wide so the two men could enter. As he brushed by her Walsh could smell her, and he tried to stop a rush of indecent memories, unsuccessfully. The boniness she'd had as a kid was gone, smoothed out. Her hazel eyes seemed a little greener than he remembered, but the same gold sparkled all through the irises.

"You're in a lot of trouble," she said with a frown, but without a shred of judgment. "Did you impersonate an FBI agent?"

He wrinkled his mouth and gave a little shrug, as if to say that was the least of it. Her frown disappeared, and even the Duke could see the wave of memory swim across her face. The nine years had disappeared. And Walsh seemed to feel it had gone too far, that somebody might get hurt if he didn't stick to the matter at hand. "Gail, I won't stay long," he said. "I need some money to get to L.A. You know I'm good for it."

She nodded. Still no judgment in her eyes. Walsh looked away, suddenly feeling ridiculous and confused. "I'm so embarrassed. See, I'm just in a jam right now." It was as if he was just talking to talk, and he looked up again and fixed on a deeper place in her eyes and said, "You look so beautiful." He tried to grin, but couldn't hide the catch in his voice.

Gail's eyes filled with tears, and she had to bite her lip. Just then the seven-year-old, who had been studying the scene from across the foyer—especially the handcuffs—sauntered over between his mother and Walsh and addressed the Duke. "You don't look much like a criminal," he said with a certain disappointment.

"I'm a white-collar criminal," the Duke replied.

Walsh was still trying to hold his ex-wife's gaze, but he was helpless to stop the tenderness in her eyes turning to fear. "Jack, you shouldn't be here," she declared urgently. "If Ted comes home, he'll arrest you. And him, too.'' She gestured pointedly toward the Duke, determined to focus them back on their real predicament.

Just the way she said the name—*Ted*—did a bad thing to his guts. He felt an absurd protectiveness toward the Duke, as if someone had just insulted his friend. A dumb and useless anger blanketed his heart. ''Arrest us?'' he retorted with huge disdain, then turned and faced the accountant. ''Then we'd *really* be in trouble, 'cause I'm a little short on bribe money.''

Gail sighed. ''Jack, don't start, please. Today is not a good day for this.''

With a short tug on the cuffs, the Duke murmured out of the side of his mouth, ''Yeah, Jack, don't start.''

But Walsh plowed ahead, puffing his chest out and bobbing his head like a fighter. ''I'm sorry my fugitive timetable doesn't coincide with your social calendar.''

Now the Duke sighed. ''I don't think she was saying that, Jack.''

''Stay out of this, Jonathan,'' warned the bounty hunter, the first time he'd ever called the accountant by his name.

''Same old Jack,'' said Gail, annoyed now, her chin jutted forward and her hands on her hips. ''Gets his feelings hurt and tries to hurt everyone around him.''

Walsh thought how unfair it was that she looked sexy even when she was pissed off. ''Gail, the last thing I need right now is one of your lectures.''

She practically shouted at him. ''I'm trying to protect you, stupid!'' The seven-year-old flinched and backed off from the group. Irrelevantly Walsh registered that Gail and Ted didn't fight too much. Couldn't be that hot a marriage then, he thought with satisfaction. ''Ted's going to be home any minute,'' Gail continued. ''Tonight's a very important night for us. We're all going out.''

Walsh was like a bull with a red flag. ''What's so special about tonight? Wait—let me guess. Graft night?''

"That's enough!" Gail shrieked.

"All right, everyone," purred the Duke, "let's not fight."

"Gail, I just need some money," Walsh said tightly, trying now to strip from his voice any feeling whatsoever. "All I gotta do is get this guy to L.A., and I'm outa this miserable business forever."

He glanced over her shoulder and saw in the doorway another Gail, just the way she'd looked when he'd met her in the tenth grade. For a second he thought he would literally pass out. Anybody—even if he wasn't her father—*anybody* would have to say she was breathtaking. Her mother's hair and eyes, a little taller maybe, but she smiled at him with his own exact smile. "Hi," said Walsh in a shaky voice, almost afraid to say her name, then needing to more than the fear. "Hi, Denise."

As Gail turned and left the foyer, Denise walked over and kissed her father on the cheek. "Hi, Daddy," she said, no awkwardness at all, as friendly as if she saw him every day. Walsh put his free arm around her, while his other hand tugged unconsciously at the cuffs. Denise locked her hands behind his back, and father and daughter squeezed very tight, their eyes clenched shut to hold the tears. His voice was the barest whisper in her ear, "You're so grown up."

They broke the embrace as Gail returned from the other room. Walsh forced himself not to look at Denise and said to his ex-wife, "I'll go now. I'm sorry."

"Here, Jack, take this," she replied, and pressed into his hand a fold of cash and a set of keys. "I only have forty dollars, but take my car. I'll tell Ted it's in the shop. We'll worry about it after you get to LA."

Mother and daughter stood next to each other, like two suns in the sky. Walsh hefted the keys in his hand and looked nakedly at Gail. "Does he take good care of you?"

She nodded. "That's all I want to know," said Walsh with a glimmer of his old brisk self. He held out his hand with the keys and money, as if daring her to take them back. "What will he say about this?"

"He'll understand."

Walsh nodded. In fact, the nod went on for a long moment, but nobody made a move to hurry him along. They all stood and waited for Walsh to finish his nod. And finally he said, "That's love."

He tugged at the Duke's wrist, and they headed out and down the brick steps. They crossed the lawn to the driveway, where a big blue LTD was parked. Walsh could have probably figured to the nickel just how many bribes it cost. He wrenched open the passenger's door, then quickly uncuffed himself, double-cuffed the Duke, and sat him down in the car. As the bounty hunter moved to go round to the driver's side, he nearly collided with Denise. He shrank a step away from her, as if he couldn't stand another encounter.

"It isn't much," she said, holding out her two cupped hands. Walsh cocked his head with curiosity, temporarily dazed, automatically reaching out with an open palm. He felt the feather softness of the bills as she laid them in his hands. "It's like baby-sitting money," she said. "Maybe two hundred dollars. No big deal."

He was shocked and pushed the money back, but she flurried his hand away with hers. Her fingers felt like a butterfly. "Please . . . Daddy," she gulped, trying to stay a grown-up, "it's the only thing I've ever asked you to do for me."

He nodded in a dream—so much to say, no time at all. He didn't dare do another thing but get in the car and go, and though she remained on the edge of the lawn to watch them drive off, neither she nor her father waved. Walsh could hardly breathe as he watched her diminish in the rearview mirror. There was nothing obnoxious at all in the Duke's next remark. "You have a beautiful daughter, Jack," he said, and Walsh nodded again, as if he'd been nodding for days. To the Duke he replied quite formally, "I'd just like to be quiet for a while."

And that's how it was for a quarter of a mile: very, very quiet. Then out of nowhere Walsh pulled a U-turn, shrieking completely around and heading back the way they'd come. The Duke said nothing. Ten seconds later they came up again on the house, where a startled Denise still stood exactly where he'd left her. His heart beat fast as he thought of another encounter, however brief. As he slowed to turn into the drive, a late-model Buick pulled up from the other direction and swung right in.

Walsh stopped across the street and watched as if it were an accident. Ted heaved out of the Buick, nattily dressed and unaware of Walsh. He threw a casual arm around Denise and led her back to the house, laughing so loud they could hear it across the street. As they disappeared into the house, Denise threw a farewell glance over her shoulder, sad and much too old for her age. When the door closed, Walsh watched the impassive front of the house in a trance. The Duke said nothing.

With a slow hand Walsh reached into his pocket and took out the wad of cash his daughter had pressed on him. He put the car in park but left it running as he got out, as if he'd forgotten the Duke was a dangerous man. He loped over to the opposite curb, where a mailbox cute as a birdhouse perched beside the driveway. Walsh yanked open the lid and stuffed the money inside. He was back in the car a moment later without a backward glance, and they were on their way.

The Duke said nothing.

Jerry grabbed the phone in Moscone's office halfway

through the first ring. He looked like he hadn't slept in a week, and he hadn't read the morning paper, though it was already almost dusk. As soon as he heard the first syllable of Walsh's voice through the static, he bawled for Eddie Moscone. The bail bondsman was in his cubicle, in the middle of a snake-oil deal with a lawyer and a criminal. Now he cut them off with a wave and swiveled his chair to the phone.

"Walsh, where *are* you?" pleaded Eddie Moscone.

"I'm in Boise, Idaho," came the reply, blurred by a hurricane of noise. Three hundred yards away in the battered van, the agents with the earphones huddled with their scribbling pencils. "No, wait a minute," Jack Walsh said, "I'm in Casper, Wyoming." The two agents looked at each other. Moscone couldn't even find a pencil. "No, wait—I'm in Anchorage, Alaska. I'm in the lobby of a Howard Johnson's. I'm wearing a pink carnation."

"What the hell are you talkin' about?" roared Eddie Moscone.

"I'm not talkin' to you, Eddie. I'm talkin' to the other guys." You could hear the grin on Walsh's face even through fifteen hundred miles of bad connection.

"What other guys?"

"Eddie, you're not payin' *attention,*" scolded Walsh. "There's these guys, see? They've prob'ly been up for three days, so like, they stink of BO. They got coffee breath worse than Jerry." In the cave of the van the two agents shifted nervously, and one of them stared at his Thermos. Walsh went merrily on. "They're real constipated, and they got terrible hemorrhoids from sitting on their asses so long . . ."

Moscone was open-mouthed. As if he was talking to a crazy person, he picked his words with the greatest care. "Hey, Walsh, just tell me—have you still got him?"

". . . And they're real easy to spot, Eddie, 'cause they

always sit in a van. They're right up the street from your office, over by Denny's. They always gotta have take-out within a hundred yards. It's a federal law.''

As Walsh chattered on, drunk on the sound of his voice, Moscone stood up and crossed to his front window. He parted the blinds and looked out on the purple dusk of Vignes Street. The van was on the corner across from Denny's, looking vaguely ashamed.

''. . . But now they're gonna have to pack up all their shit and go home, because I'm onto them!'' Walsh crowed with vindictive triumph. ''You dumb fucks! I'm not usin' this line anymore!''

The pencils in the agents' hands went limp. They couldn't even bear to look at each other, and they certainly weren't going to write all this crap down. It was going to be bad enough telling their superiors that Jack Walsh had managed to smoke them out long-distance.

''Hey, Eddie,'' Walsh called to the poor bail bondsman, who was drowning in paranoia now. ''Go to Denny's. I'll call you in two minutes. They can't run a tap that fast.''

''Yo,'' said Moscone, slamming the phone down. And he sprinted out of his cubicle, ignoring the lawyer and his piddling assault-with-deadly, running out past a dazed and frustrated Jerry. As he trotted down Vignes Street his heart was pounding so bad he thought he was having a coronary, but he goddamn well wasn't going to die before he found out if Walsh still had his precious cargo.

He cut a wide swath around the offending van and went barreling into Denny's. The lady manager who'd fed him for a decade was already holding out the receiver when Eddie Moscone came puffing up to the register. With quaking hands he cradled it to his ear and panted into the phone, which apparently worked as a kind of hello, for Walsh started speaking right away.

"Eddie, I need you to wire me five hundred to Western Union in Amarillo, Texas. Pronto."

All the tension and the waiting exploded from Eddie Moscone. "What do you need with five hundred bucks on a *bus?*" he bawled, not caring who heard him at Denny's. The regulars all thought he was out of his gourd, anyway. "And why the hell aren't you on a plane like a normal person?"

That grin came through the phone again, wide as the Cheshire Cat. "Did it ever occur to you, Eddie, that I'm a pro and I might have my reasons? We had to scrap the bus. We're in a car now, and we only got enough cash to get to Texas."

"What do you think this is, Walsh, a fuckin' sight-seeing trip? What happened to the *plane?*"

"What can I tell ya, Eddie. He don't like to fly."

Poor Eddie Moscone blew his last gasket. "He don't like to fly?" he repeated in shrill disbelief, stomping back and forth. Even the waitresses were afraid to approach the register. "What the fuck does that mean?! You gotta be here in two days, or we're *all* up shit's creek! Why are you doin' this to me, Jack?"

Walsh spoke like a man who had all the cards in his hand. "I swear to God, Eddie," he sneered from the middle of nowhere, "don't start with me now or I'll shoot him and dump him in the swamp. I'm in no fuckin' mood. Just send me the money and I'll have him back in time. Over and out."

Walsh had been hanging up on Moscone for days now, so at least he was getting used to it. His anger seemed to deflate like a pricked balloon as the dial tone rang in his ear. He trudged out of Denny's and back up Vignes Street to his office, not even noticing that the rusty van had moved a pathetic fifty yards, so it was half-hidden by a curbside clump of oleander. If nothing else, Eddie Moscone

was determined not to appear out of control in front of
Jerry. He assumed a strutting pose as he entered the office.

"Hey, Jerry," he said brusquely, "wire five hundred to
Walsh in Amarillo, Texas." The flatulent assistant nodded
and reached for the phone. With a cunning smile Moscone
added, "Maybe you ought to see if you can't get Dorfler
down there, too."

Poor Eddie Moscone just didn't see how endlessly he set
the wheels in motion. Jerry did what he was told, of
course, placing the call to Western Union while the bondsman went back to assault-with-deadly. But two minutes
later Jerry was puffing down Vignes Street himself, heading for his trusty phone booth on the corner. And in the
battered van under the oleander, the battered agents perked
up again.

It was the first squeak of early morning, milky rose in
the east and streaks of purple cloud shooting the dome of
the Texas sky. The LTD was covered with grime like a
boxcar as it rolled up to a pancake house surrounded by
eighteen-wheelers. When Walsh and the Duke dragged out
of the car they were glassy-eyed with fatigue and in very
bad need of a shave. As they arched the kinks out of their
backs, they looked as if they'd ridden to Amarillo on a
freight train, in a car with a load of cattle. They did not
speak. Finally the Duke appeared to be talked out.

The pancake house was in the kidney-counter spaceship
mode of the fifties. As they headed in, the Duke held his
hands together piously to hide the cuffs. Bacon and flap-
jacks sizzled lusciously on the hot griddle. The bounty
hunter and his prey took seats at the end of the counter.
Across from them was a young ranch hand in a denim
jacket and thermal shirt, smearing a slice of toast in a wide
arc round his plate, scooping up the last of his eggs and

grits. The bellies of Walsh and the Duke growled in unison.

Damned if Walsh could figure out why he always got hungry immediately after he went broke. He'd go days on coffee and Camels, then run out of money and be suddenly ravenous. A tart and worldly waitress padded up to the new arrivals, her jet-black hair spilling wildly from the boundaries of a rubber band and two poodle barrettes. She raised her eyebrows helpfully and drawled as sleepy as Texas, "What can I do for you, boys?"

Walsh's smile was thin and courteous. "Two coffees," he said without inflection.

"I prefer herbal tea," interjected the Duke with elaborate ducal dignity. Then he turned to Walsh beside him, taking care not to lower his voice. "As a bounty hunter, are you licensed to starve your victims?"

Walsh let the remark pass, and the waitress wasn't impressed, having served every outlaw in six counties. When she sidled away to the java urn, Walsh tilted his wrist and checked his Timex. "In twenty minutes we'll have five hundred bucks," he said with cool dispassion, though his stomach growled like a tiger. "Then I'll buy you a nice, juicy steak."

"I don't eat meat," responded the accountant archly. "It's filled with carcinogens and steroids."

Walsh scowled, weary to death of the Duke's fruitcake dos and don'ts. He actually couldn't remember liking anyone who didn't eat meat. Not that he purposely avoided such purist types; he just couldn't remember ever liking anyone who couldn't pig out at a barbecue. And he longed for a steak himself, so bad that his palms itched.

"You know, Jonathan, you're a very smart guy," he said with elaborate casualness. "You know absolutely everything about absolutely everything. I never seen anything like it—I mean that. Traveling with you is like having my own portable *Encyclopedia Britannica*." He gave his prisoner a slow and foxy grin, as the accountant grabbed a napkin from the holder and rubbed the counter clean. "But I'll tell ya somethin," Walsh went on, "you don't know enough to stay out of other people's business. How could you mess with a guy like Serano? Sounds like the kinda thing a jerk would do who don't know nothin'."

"I had a way out of this," observed the Duke, crisp with self-esteem.

"Oh, really?" This ought to be good.

"Yup. I was going to put all of Serano's records on computer disks, kind of like an insurance policy. I figured I could always trade them for my life if things got rough."

The waitress set the cups down. Walsh plopped half a cup of cream and two sugars in his coffee. The Duke, austere as a hermit, stirred his pale yellow lemon-herb tea with a lazy spoon. As Walsh slurped his coffee he tried not to stare at a double-fudge cake on a stand three feet away. "But there's a million easier ways to steal money," he said. "Why didn't you just leave him alone? You can't win with a guy like that."

"Why didn't you just ignore the corruption in the police department?" retorted the Duke quietly.

Walsh tensed, offended by the comparison. "Because I couldn't live with myself, that's why." End of story. Walsh peered over his cup out the wall of glass, where nothing broke the monotonous tawny flatness of the landscape.

"Well, that's how I felt, Jack. I wasn't some mob accountant, you know. I thought I was working for a legitimate business." Walsh turned and stared at him. He wouldn't have thought it possible before meeting Jonathan Mardukas, but now he had to admit that if anyone could not know, it was this man with the improbable title. "When I found out I was managing accounts that were really fronts for Serano, I just couldn't sit back and do nothing. Now, could I?''

Walsh gave a short grunt, but there was respect in it. ''So you decided to take what didn't belong to you.''

The Duke laughed dryly. ''Jack, I gave practically all of it to charity. How can you take the side of a mobster, a guy that sells heroin to school kids?''

Walsh blinked at him in disbelief, still trying to take in the charity part. The Duke was priceless, a cross between H&R Block and St. Francis of Assisi. ''I'm not taking his side,'' Walsh replied curtly.

''You're taking his side if you're not taking mine.''

Why did he always have to stir things up—demanding a human being, reminding, insisting. Couldn't he ever leave anything alone? ''I'm not taking *anybody's* side,'' Walsh hissed with greater force. ''I've got nothing to do with this.'' The minute he said them, the words tasted like the bottom of a bird cage. Abruptly he checked his Timex again and growled like a man with a hangover, ''Time to go.''

He poured out the last pool of his change on the counter and slipped off the stool. Meekly the Duke fell in step beside him, but, of course, he had not had the last word yet. ''Why do you wear that old watch?'' he asked, maddeningly innocent.

''I'll tell you that when I know you better,'' said Walsh with an edge of mockery, but the edge was blunt. He reached over and grabbed the chain that linked the cuffs, tugging the Duke to follow him. It was a completely unnecessary thing to do, and the Duke gave a small gasp of discomfort. But as Walsh led his prisoner out the door, it was clear that no one escaped unhurt.

West Eighth Street in Amarillo is as blank as they get in Texas: flat, gray, vaguely industrial, abandoned streetcar tracks down the middle. Western Union had been there since the Alamo, before the streetlights and telephone poles. A block away from the telegraph office waited the black Chrysler, with Tony Daruvo groggy and cross-eyed at the wheel. *This shit has got to stop,* he thought in his more lucid moments.

Every distance Walsh and the Duke had covered—by train and bus—Tony had done in his own car. In expenses alone this trip would wipe him out, if Serano didn't do it first. In addition to which, if Joey Ribuffo didn't stop jiggling his knee and chomping those corn nuts, Tony was going to tear the retard apart.

"You know what we should get?" asked Joey, who was wide awake and never seemed to require any sleep at all, as long as he had his junk-food fix. "One of those little trays that you keep in the car, so you don't spill food and drinks all over the place and stuff."

Tony Daruvo could feel his face contort into an Oliver Hardy slow-burn. Yeah, he thought, it would probably be real funny to *someone*. And then, suddenly Walsh and Mardukas were there, walking across West Eighth, wrist to wrist. Tony jumped on the starter and peeled out with a squeal of rubber. The Chrysler covered the block in two seconds, and Tony and Joey were out on the curb surrounding Walsh and the Duke like a couple of ravenous hunting dogs.

Walsh saw them and froze, automatically bracing his mind for the shots and the dying, even though the two hoods hadn't yet taken their guns from their pockets. The accountant gave out with a small whimper and leaned closer to the bounty hunter. If they didn't shoot right away, thought Walsh, they wouldn't shoot at all. Tony Daruvo seemed to be on the same wavelength as he snarled in Walsh's face, "Don't fuckin' move, asshole. I don't wanna kill you."

Walsh could feel the Duke's body next to him relax, but Tony Daruvo as always saved the best part for last. He turned to the accountant and said with enormous satisfaction, "I just want you." *Dead* was understood.

Now the Duke began to hyperventilate. Walsh was trying to think quick, groping for an exit line, when out of the alley beside the telegraph office stepped Max Dorfler. He had a .45 cocked in his hand. Walsh wasn't sure whether this was the good news or the bad news. "Drop 'em," barked Dorfler.

Tony's and Joey's shoes made a high crunching sound as they slowly pivoted around. "You heard me, drop 'em," Dorfler repeated, not having the kind of imagination that can change clichés in midstream. Tony and Joey slowly pulled out their pieces and tossed them at Dorfler's feet. "Who the fuck are *you* guys?" Dorfler inquired, more bewildered than angry.

"Yeah, well, who the fuck are you?" Tony Daruvo parroted, not known for being so wildly original himself.

Dorfler stepped up to Tony and smacked a vicious upper-cut to his jaw with the butt of the .45. Tony crashed and ate the pavement. Walsh was starting to feel that at any moment the Duke would crawl into his pocket. Joey Ribuffo stared at his partner prone on the pavement, then shook his head at Dorfler in slow disbelief. "You're dead," said Joey. "You know who you're messin' with?" He wasn't bragging, just stating an awesome fact.

"No," sneered Dorfler, "why don't you tell me about it. And make sure you speak into the microphone." To punctuate the last word he whacked the butt of the gun into Joey's mouth. Joey pitched backwards and hit the ground, out cold. Until just this moment Walsh had always seen Dorfler's particular brand of evil as relatively impotent. Dorfler turned to his fellow bounty hunter, his face gray with rage. "Gimme the keys to the cuffs."

"Sure, Max," said Walsh. In a second the keys were dangling in Walsh's fingers, and the next second they were pitched irretrievably, jingling merrily against the concrete, then lost in the nether world beneath a sewer grate. "Looks like a package deal to me," declared Walsh with a shrug and a shit-eating grin.

"Front row, Jack!" enthused the Duke, who would've applauded if he'd had both hands.

"So we got us a coupla comedians, huh?" said Dorfler contemptuously. "All right, both of you, let's go." He tried to make it sound as much like his own idea as possible. Waving them into the street, he marched them across to his Cadillac and scooted them into the front seat like a pair of wayward kids. When Dorfler got in on the driver's side, he managed to start the car and steer with one hand, keeping his other hand wrapped around the .45 on his knee. The Duke, sitting right beside him, took care not to let their knees touch.

"Who the hell *were* those guys?" Dorfler asked Walsh, more casual now, bounty hunter to bounty hunter.

Walsh guffawed. "Oh, Maxie, you done it this time," he said. "Those were hired killers back there."

"Hired to kill who?" asked Dorfler, almost offended, as if somebody should have asked his permission.

"Him," said Walsh, pointing to the Duke between them. "Hired by Jimmy Serano," he added, spilling the name one slow syllable at a time.

"Oh, no!" groaned Dorfler. "What do they want to kill *this* putz for?" He hitched a thumb in the Duke's direction.

"Maxie, don't you read the newspapers?"

The Duke put his head in his hands. "I can't take this anymore," he whimpered, just short of a blubber.

"You shut up," scolded Walsh, then leaned across to Dorfler. "How did *you* know where we were? Did Moscone put you on this?"

"Of course Moscone put me on this," Dorfler replied dismissively, flicking his pinkie finger. He was brooding about something else, calculating in another direction. His toupee seemed to be percolating on top of his head.

"That no-good son-of-a-bitch!" bawled Walsh, thumping the dash with the heel of his hand. "We got a contract!" But as soon as he said it, he knew how naive and ridiculous it sounded. A contract with Eddie Moscone and fifty cents would buy you a bad cup of coffee.

Dorfler shrugged. "He called me in Pittsburgh. He said you were fuckin' it up."

"I'm not fuckin' it up! Don't you dare tell me how to do my goddamned job!"

"Jack, you were s'posed to be in LA two days ago." The disdain fairly dripped from Dorfler's voice. Between his superiority and Walsh's air of offended pride, they were like two bad neighbors brawling over a backyard fence.

"Yeah, well, you listen good, Max. I'm half thinkin' not to turn him in at all, just to watch Moscone go down the drain."

The Duke chimed in, "Now that's an *excellent* idea."

"Who the fuck is talkin' to you?" bellowed Walsh, giving a tug to the cuffs. Nothing he did or said was exempt from this damned accountant. He couldn't even belch without subjecting it to the Duke's two cents.

"He's not yours to take in anymore," said Dorfler.

And then the car began to throb, a hard "phutt" slapping the air around it like a giant lawn sprinkler. It got much louder very fast, and Walsh looked out the side window and saw the lumbering shadow pass across the ochre flatland. "Oh, Christ," said Walsh quietly, never hearing that sound without recalling Nam. He patted the Zippo in his pocket for luck.

"All right, who's this?" asked Dorfler in a pugnacious

voice, ducking his head out the window, trying to spot the chopper. It was directly behind and above them, holding tight to the Cadillac's blind spot.

"It's either Serano or the feds," Walsh replied with grisly resignation.

A hailstorm of bullets peppered the road all around them like a small, demented storm. The sharpshooters in the helicopter were using M-16s. Dorfler gripped his steering wheel with both hands, knuckles taut, as if the Cadillac had suddenly become a raft in white water.

"Serano," said Walsh, scarcely missing a beat.

The chopper hovered above them grimly, tight as a magnet. The sound of beating wind was deafening. There were two marksmen, one on either side of the bubble, leaning out with one foot on the runner. The M-16s were locked to their shoulders, and they strafed the road below like a battleground.

The back window of the Cadillac exploded in a burst of shards. The Duke buried his head in Walsh's shoulder as the bounty hunter tried to cover him, instinctively protecting his ace in the hole. The two bounty hunters were hollering at each other, but neither could make out a word over the roar of the wind and the gunfire. A rain of bullets came through the roof. Walsh felt the sting of the air beside his ear as a slap of lead embedded itself in the headrest.

Then the hood exploded, jackknifing toward the windshield so Dorfler couldn't see at all. As he veered back and forth off the shoulder of the road, kicking dust like a road runner, the hood broke free and sailed over the roof. Dorfler jammed the brakes like a man who was putting his foot down at last. Every wheel burned an inch of rubber as the Caddie rocketed to a halt, the chopper whirling on ahead and banking in a wide arc.

As it started back toward them, tantalized like a shark

who wanted seconds, Dorfler gunned the accelerator once again. The battered Caddie zoomed beneath the oncoming chopper and gained perhaps a quarter mile as the chopper roared harmlessly over their heads. The sharpshooters couldn't get a bead on the target till the helicopter had banked again. Walsh was screaming to get Dorfler's attention, but the driver seemed mesmerized by his dodging maneuver, ready to jam the brakes again. As if they could spend the whole day lurching across Texas.

"This is bullshit!" shouted Walsh. "We're sittin' ducks, Maxie!" He leaned across the Duke, who was staring goggle-eyed with disbelief at the oncoming road. Walsh shrieked in Dorfler's ear, "Get off the fuckin' road!"

The chopper was on top of them again, the gunners strafing the ground below with a taste of scorched earth. A bullet pinged off the outside mirror, and the driver's side window disintegrated. A few hundred yards ahead loomed a bridge out of an Erector Set, and an eighteen-wheeler was trundling across it in their direction, with barely a car's width to spare. All they could see from the Caddie was bridge and truck, immovable object and irresistible force, all in one. The three men in the car saw at the same instant that they were heading straight into a nightmare.

They would have had to be in the chopper to see the gorge below the bridge, four hundred feet from the rim to the rapids below, like a rip in the planet. Dorfler's hands were frozen to the wheel, steering straight ahead as if he'd lost the will to dodge, on course like a kamikaze. The helicopter skimmed and butchered the air above them. The eighteen-wheeler hadn't slowed an inch since Dallas, and it wasn't going to start now. It had no room to swerve on the bridge. If chicken was the game they were going to play, then the Caddie was going to lose in spades.

"Look out!" shrieked the Duke, but nobody listened— not the semi, not the chopper, not Dorfler.

For the longest second all three vehicles stayed on course, pointing to zero, roaring at each other like a trio of prehistoric beasts. Then Walsh threw his body across the Duke's and grabbed the wheel with his good hand, trying to tear it from Dorfler, who held it like a vise. They were so close the Duke could have counted the dead flies on the truck's wide grill as it came exploding off the bridge. And just then Dorfler must have flinched a hair, as Walsh felt a millimeter's play in the wheel, and the car veered at the last gasp, slamming through the guardrail.

For an instant they were as airborne as the wheeling chopper. Walsh felt his gut heave into his throat and the cuff dig into his wrist as the Duke flailed his arms. They landed with a sickening crunch on the steeply graded slope of the gorge, sideswiping boulders and cottonwood trees as they began the long career. They could feel the shrubs and underbrush whacking at the belly of the car. The Duke had been screaming a one-note scream like an opera singer ever since they left the road, but it was a mouse's noise beside the avalanche all around them. *They* were the avalanche.

Walsh braced himself for the inevitable crash, feet against the dashboard. But somehow Dorfler managed to keep swerving and dodging on his blown-out tires, barely missing a sickening array of rocks and tree trunks. And all the way, Dorfler chattered like a spider monkey. "Okay, okay, I got it," he said to no one in particular, as he hotdogged a trail by the seat of his pants. With an agonized groan, a heavy, jagged limb walloped the passenger's door, denting it in six inches. "Hang in, relax!" cried Dorfler. "I got it!"

The boiling rapids loomed closer and closer as they plunged the lower slope, riding on their axles. Then, as if the god that was playing this game had suddenly had enough, the Caddie slammed to a halt, wedging itself in the stony crotch between two boulders. The white-water stream was so close that the Caddie was instantly doused with spray, and, as if by instinct, the windshield wipers started thwocking back and forth. The scraping, crunching sounds of the downhill slide had stopped, but there was nothing so simple as silence. The stream roared. The whirring chopper banked over the bridge and headed into the gorge toward the paralyzed car.

In the front seat the three men were tangled like a pretzel. Dorfler scrambled to pull out his .45, but in the general melee it tumbled to the floor. The Duke, who was hanging with his head down off the seat, scooped up the gun and struggled back into place between the two bounty hunters. "Nobody move," he said in his best Bogart twang, swinging the .45 back and forth between Dorfler and Walsh.

"Oh, for Christ's sake, gimme that," Walsh said irritably, grabbing the gun right out of the accountant's hand. Dorfler lunged across the Duke and snatched the gun from Walsh. "That's mine," he said with his last gasp of pride, trying not to think of his poor, beloved Caddie.

The car doors were pinned shut by the boulders. The only way out was through the windows. Walsh and the Duke, their wrists raw at the cuffs, scrambled out on the passenger's side, while Dorfler evacuated through the shattered rear windshield. As they stood shakily on the sloping ground, trying to get their bearings, the gallant Duke tried to brush the bits of broken glass from his clothes. Walsh squinted up into the sun and saw the chopper bearing down, the sharpshooters hanging out of the bubble, M-16s poised.

Instantly Walsh tackled the Duke and sent them both rolling into a clump of shrubbery. The sudden rain of bullets spit little bursts of dust from the ground all around them, as Dorfler shimmied into the shrubbery after them, one hand firmly planted on his hairpiece. As the chopper roared closer, Walsh ducked in under a low granite outcropping, dragging the Duke in after him. Dorfler didn't seem to notice the spray of bullets everywhere. He knelt like a dimwit hero and fired his .45 at the chopper hovering overhead. Only when the clip was empty did he reluctantly leave the field of battle and scramble in under the ledge beside Walsh and the Duke.

Icy calm as a battle surgeon, Walsh reached into his pocket and pulled out a small key. Then he grabbed the Duke's wrist to unlock the cuffs. "I thought you threw those out!" yelled Dorfler, eyes wide with righteous indignation.

"Always check the evidence, Max. Those were my car keys." Walsh turned to the Duke and saw his wide smile of impending freedom. Even as the cuff fell away from the accountant's wrist, Walsh pointed up in the sky and said, "Hey, they're not after me." The Duke's smile vanished, and his face went queasy. "Just kiddin'," Walsh added with a broad wink.

It was starting to feel like the Alamo. Dorfler tossed to Walsh the .45 he'd taken from the hit man back in Amarillo. Then he shoved a new clip in his own gun, and the two men ducked out from under the narrow overhang just as the chopper made another pass. A lucky shot of Walsh's hit the glass bubble at the pilot's feet, exploding a gaping hole in it. Again the chopper swung angrily away and came around in a wide circle, determined as a hornet. In a panic, the Duke sprinted out into the open, making for the boulders by the car.

He was the prize game. As the chopper came hammering in again for another strafing, the sharpshooters ignored the pair of bounty hunters and narrowed a bead on the Duke. Bullets began to explode around him as he clambered among the rocks, disoriented by the sudden wetness in the air. By the time Walsh realized his prisoner was no longer huddling behind him, the Duke was disappearing into the mist beyond the rocks. The chopper sailed over the bounty hunters' heads, honing in for the kill. Dorfler and Walsh sprinted after it.

It was a hardball game of cat and mouse as the Duke inched onto a narrow ledge, wet to the skin from the spray already, trying not to look down. The chopper hovered above him like a flying dragon. The marksmen opened fire, and the accountant flinched at the high pinging sound of the bullets on granite. Walsh and Dorfler were rock-climbing their way toward him, shouting at him to come back. Then the Duke tried to look over his shoulder to see where the chopper was. His neatly buffed accountant's wingtip slipped on the mossy ledge, and he tumbled back-wards into the boiling current.

Walsh would've dived in right after him, but the M-16s wouldn't quit and kept him pinned in the rocks. He turned and groaned at Dorfler in frustration. "Son of a bitch!" The spray from the rapids splashed his face like tears. "Well, Max, there goes a hundred grand!"

Dorfler's eyebrows shot up. "You're getting a *hundred?*"

"Why? What was he gonna pay you?" Suddenly it didn't seem to matter that bullets were ricocheting all around them.

"Twenty-five," replied Dorfler, wounded and deflated, like a guy with a lottery ticket just one digit off the jackpot.

The marksman on the left runner blade of the chopper suddenly pointed to the stream below as he barked at the pilot. Walsh followed his finger and saw the Duke clinging to a logjam, trying to keep his head above the nightmarish current. The chopper nosed in closer to the stream, and the marksman leveled his M-16 and fired. Walsh suddenly realized that the helicopter was practically dangling its tail rotor in his face. "Maxie, gimme another clip!" he shouted.

Dorfler hesitated, but Walsh had the eyes of a man you couldn't say no to. He held out the clip. Walsh jammed it into the butt of his pistol and scurried along the rocky bank, as the sharpshooters swept the stream with wave after wave of firepower. The Duke was bobbing and half underwater, so he made a very dicey target. Walsh was right below the chopper's open belly and tail, and he crouched with the easy grace of a Sioux with a longbow. He raised his arm and sighted in, then grinned that slow grin of his as he murmured, "Say goodnight, Gracie."

He fired off five shots, his arm like a rock. It wasn't the sound of his own gunfire that left him looking so blank, it was the suddenness of being back in time. In fact, he could have sworn later it was the smell of the metal exploding, as the tail rotor burst in a bloom of fragments, razoring the ground below. If you wanted to forget a past like Walsh's, it was probably best to stay out of a firefight with a chopper.

But that only lasted a second. The next second the chopper was a dragon blinded and mad with pain. It swooped so low that Walsh and Dorfler hit the deck and ate dirt, then it reeled upward again and seemed to pivot in the air, taking a last look at the sky. One of the marksmen hung from the doorway, the rifle still in his hand. Then the chopper gave out with a deafening whine, swinging itself like a scorpion as it descended toward the wall of the high gorge.

It seemed to touch the cliff and erupt in a fireball, as if it involved no crash at all. The fire rolled upward, away from the tumbling, charred skeleton of the chopper. Shrapnel screamed in a hundred directions. Dorfler nearly danced with pleasure. "Goddamn, Jack! You did it!" He turned and opened his arms to Walsh like a prodigal son.

Walsh smiled, took a step toward him, and punched him square in the jaw, grunting at the crack of his own fingers. Dorfler saw stars and fell back against the trunk of the Caddie, then slumped to the ground, out cold. Walsh went for his left front pocket and pulled out the cuffs and the keys. He pulled up Dorfler's wrist, cuffed it with an indecent thrill of satisfaction, then dragged him around to the door, cuffing him to the handle. As he flung the keys over his shoulder into the water, Max Dorfler was coming out of it and shot him a cross-eyed look.

"See you in L.A., Max!" he called with a cheery wave, then turned and leaped in a kind of swan dive into the raging white of the stream.

9

THE FORCE OF the snowmelt current barreled the Duke downstream, somersaulting madly. He'd pop up in one place, then sink for a while and pop up again like a bathtub toy. Each time he resurfaced he gasped desperately for a gulp of air, but the water was already numbing his body. He no longer felt the bottom rocks and the flotsam debris as they tore at his clothes and scraped his skin. Or he felt them, but they didn't hurt anymore. Somewhere in the back of his methodical mind, he knew this was a symptom of hypothermia.

Every time he bobbed he could see a small, natural dam at a bend in the rapids ahead, jutting out four or five feet from the bank of the stream. It was only a battered log and some loose branches that had gotten caught between some rocks, but it seemed like paradise itself just now. The Duke clawed the water, making his way toward it. Fate and a shrug of the current led him to it more than his frantic swimming, but suddenly he rammed the logjam and spun in the whirlpool before it. Heart pounding with joy, he gripped the log with both hands and began to shin his way to the bank.

Meanwhile, just upstream, Walsh was bouncing along

on the same toboggan run. He stayed limp and went with the drift much more than the Duke—sometimes what-the-fuck was exactly the right attitude—and managed not to get scraped and pummeled. Ahead he could see the Duke inching his way along the log to safety, but fate and the current weren't so generous to Walsh. As he raced by the logjam he just managed to grab a branch, but it only slowed him for a second. Suddenly the whole bundle dislodged, dragging the Duke back in and sending both men rocketing on.

They were clinging to the same, useless tree limb as the white water shifted gears into a frenzy. "Goddamnit, I was almost safe!" bellowed the Duke in a fury.

As they rode the tree limb like drowning kittens, they saw a small mountain of water exploding through a narrow gorge between two boulders. They pinballed their way through the chute, and the tree limb managed to lodge like a brace between the rocks. The Duke was on the upstream side, bent double over the limb as the water cascaded over his back in a huge crystal fan. The luckless Walsh was on the downstream end, his arms clutching the limb and feeling as if they were pulling out of their sockets.

"I'm slipping!" he screamed. "Gimme your hand!"

They stared eye to eye, their faces a bare two feet from each other. "Promise you'll let me go!" shouted the Duke in response, trying not to sound sadistic.

"Fuck you!" Walsh retorted with a gurgle, swallowing a gallon of river water.

The Duke looked genuinely regretful. "You're making it very hard for me to do the right thing, Jack," he said. A clump of rotted leaves smashed into Walsh's face. The relentless current pulled one of his freezing hands from the limb, a finger at a time.

"All right, I'll let you go! I swear!"

Immediately the Duke reached an arm across the limb

and gripped the bounty hunter's elbow. With a strength that was surprisingly herculean, he pulled Walsh over the limb in one great heave, and the two men scrambled for the boulder. They had barely gotten a hold on the rock when the tree limb broke free and headed down the jagged falls. Hand over hand they helped each other across the boulder and onto the bank, where they lay for a moment side by side like two beached whales, drenched to the core and panting.

"Where's Dorfler?" gasped the Duke at last, his head resting on crossed arms. In his tattered clothes he looked like Robinson Crusoe.

"He's watchin' the car," Walsh replied dryly. He came up on one elbow and held the Duke squarely with his eyes. "Thanks for saving me," he said, the passion of the words no less intense for the smile that was already crinkling his mouth.

"Thanks for letting me go," the Duke replied, brimming with camaraderie.

"Uh huh." Walsh stood up and shook the water from his hair, shivering at the clamminess of his clothes. "I'll let you go, all right," he said, reaching into his pocket for the handcuffs. The accountant actually began to chuckle, anticipating a Walshian joke—"just kiddin'." In one continuous move Walsh seemed about to chuck the cuffs in the river, then swooped down and clicked them fast on the Duke's wrists. The playfulness on the Duke's face curdled into a scowl. "I'll let you go the second you're in the L.A. County Jail."

The Duke made sputtering sounds of protest, rabid with disbelief. "But I just saved your life!"

"I already thanked you for that, Jonathan," the bounty hunter replied. "Please—don't let's get started on 'fair.' I wouldn't want to lose my lunch." And he gave the cuffs a yank and pulled the accountant to his feet. They began the long trudge up the side of the gorge. Fortunately, they were both too exhausted to walk and argue at the same time. They looked more and more like a couple of bums who'd boarded the wrong freight car.

An antique crop duster was tethered beside a collapsing tin barn, its propeller creaking uneasily in the withering West Texas wind. It was the wind that turned everything in the Panhandle yellow, endlessly twisting itself into lazy dust devils. As far as the eye could see the earth was scorched and useless, preview of coming attractions for the end of the world. The dust devils rose and fell fitfully across the sunburned barnyard. A crippled old sedan on blocks. A sagging porch with a hand-lettered sign: GENERAL STORE AND FEED.

It wasn't exactly a town, but it was the best they were going to do. A dilapidated pickup turned off the road in a cloud of dust and slid to a stop beside the porch. In the bed of the truck, along with two goats, were Walsh and the Duke. Their clothes had dried like stiff cardboard, and the dust from the road had covered them with a grimy film. When the truck stopped, they grunted their way past the bleating goats and climbed down, the Duke groaning from all the bruises of the river rocks.

Two Indians got out of the cab of the truck. The driver was a tall man with a waist-length ponytail of blue-black hair that shone like gunmetal in the hot sun. The other was a barrel-bellied, thick-featured man in a punk crew cut and a Harley-Davidson T-shirt. They had scarcely exchanged a word with their two passengers since they picked them up on the road a couple of hours before.

Walsh looked at the bleak general store and the straggle of dilapidated houses that edged the road for a hundred yards on either side. When he grinned, the dust mask on his face cracked. "You know, if there's one thing I've learned on this trip,'' he said, ''it's what a beautiful country we got here.'' He turned to the tall Indian. ''I'll bet you guys must be pretty pissed off you lost it.''

The two Indians looked at Walsh as if he were not there. The accountant seemed to cringe in his shoes, as if he wanted to give a speech on Indian rights. The screen door opened, and a towering man in a cowboy hat stepped out of the general store onto the porch—Indian, too, eagle-eyed as the chief on the buffalo nickel. He gazed disdainfully at the two dust-covered tramps, faintly smelling of goat. Altogether the three red men seemed to have elevated silence to a profound and highly communicative art form.

''Just kiddin','' said Walsh, grinning like a mangy yellow dog. He held up his wrist and the Duke's, shaking the cuffs like a bad joke on himself. ''My friend here's so hungry he could eat one o' them goats. But first I gotta make a collect call.''

''Ain't got no phone,'' observed the chief impassively.

The tall one addressed the bounty hunter, speaking carefully and slowly, as if he were addressing an interplanetary visitor. ''You come with us back to the reservation,'' he said. ''There's a phone in the bureau office.''

Walsh stretched his neck in his mud-caked collar. ''What bureau would that be?''

''Indian affairs,'' said the one in the Harley-Davidson shirt.

''Oh, yeah, that one,'' Walsh replied with evident relief. Wordlessly the two young braves followed the chief into the store to get supplies. The Duke looked around at the tin barn, where a girl was casting grain to a small flock of chickens. His eyes lingered on the crop duster plane, as if he were about to make a lyrical remark. Walsh tugged the cuffs, determined not to hear any effusions about the native American soul. ''C'mon, Jonathan,'' he said, stepping up on the rusty bumper of the pickup. "Your goat misses you."

"Is this going to upset me?" Mosely asked Perry as the young subagent sprinted in with a teletype page. Mosely rubbed his huge hands over his exhausted face. They'd been working out of a piss pot of an office at the FBI complex in Chicago for most of a long, aimless day.

"I think it's safe to say that, sir," Perry responded crisply, handing the page to his boss.

At exactly that moment, Tony Daruvo and Joey Ribuffo were walking gloomily toward the front entrance of McCarran Airport in Vegas. Joey stopped once to try a dollar slot machine, and Tony punched his head to keep him walking forward. It had the horrible feeling of the last mile as they came out into the throbbing desert sun. Immediately Serano's black limousine with the smoked windows glided up to the curb, a stretch monster that always reminded Tony of Darth Vader and the Death Star.

A chauffeur in a Nazi-brown uniform clumped around and relieved them of their bags, swinging the rear door open into the lion's den. Tony gave Joey a brutal look, making it clear that he didn't want to hear a peep out of the retard. Then they ducked in and took the jump seats. Serano sat like a pasha on the plush rear seat, Sid Lyman beside him. Nobody said hello to anybody as the limo slung back into traffic.

"What's the problem with you guys?" said Jimmy Serano quietly, almost like he really cared.

"Hey, Mr. Serano, what can I tell ya?" retorted Tony Daruvo with a strained chuckle. "It's been bad luck all the way down the line." He could feel Joey's knee beside him begin to bob up and down, and he had to suppress a desire to throw him out on his ear. "Plus this guy Walsh is pretty good, Mr. Serano," Tony added. "He's no piece o' cake."

"Well, if he's so fuckin' good," said Serano, "maybe I oughta hire *him* to hit *you*."

His fat lips were cold and bloodless as an eel. Joey Ribuffo chortled at Serano's joke, but nobody else seemed to think it was very funny. They sat there tensely, two facing two, till finally Sid Lyman leaned forward to speak. A head shorter than Tony Daruvo, Sid could still look down on a guy, even from below. He'd always treated Tony nice, but it was the kind of nice that could leave you with a switchblade in your gut. "Is any of this going to come back to him?" asked Sid, tossing his head in Serano's direction.

"None of it," Tony replied with passionate vehemence. "We rented the chopper in Detroit. Cash—no trace."

"Yeah, like it's five times removed from you, Mr. Serano," Joey blurted out. "Like, you're totally clear."

Serano exploded. "I'm clear of shit!" he bellowed, so loud the chauffeur could hear him through the bulletproof window between the seats. "He's still out there! So what am I clear of?" Nobody tried to hazard a guess. Joey sank into himself and fingered the Cracker Jack whistle in his pocket. Tony tried to look like a proper hit man, tough and impassive and awaiting his next order. Serano banged the intercom button. "Pull the fuck over," he roared at the chauffeur.

Instantly the limo stopped on a dime at the curb. Serano jerked a thumb, indicating that Tony and Joey should haul ass. Lyman took a breath to protest, as if there was something more to be negotiated, but Serano silenced the lawyer with a bulldog's snarl. Sheepishly Joey and Tony slunk from the jump seats and stepped out onto the curb. Serano leaned out and spoke in a voice that gave out death sentences as casually as traffic tickets.

"I have no interest whatsoever in seeing the two of you alive again," he said, "unless you have the accountant. Is that perfectly clear, or do I gotta draw you a map of the cemetery?''

Tony and Joey bobbed their heads, and the limo lurched away. Joey looked plaintively at Tony, as if he'd missed a connection somewhere. ''I don't get it,'' he said. ''How do we get our luggage back?''

The pickup drove for an hour across the desert wastes of the reservation, kicking up dust that shrouded man and goat alike. Finally they came to a group of ratty houses strung along the road on either side, comprising a shaky and indifferent village. The Indian Affairs office was in an ugly concrete building that reeked of government inefficiency and confusion. The pickup stopped just long enough for Walsh and the Duke to climb out, then headed off up a side road among the houses, children and dogs running along behind.

Walsh and the Duke stared at each other in continuing disbelief at the state of each other's tattered disarray. The office half of the building was already closed for the day. The other side was a kind of social hall, with a couple of pool tables and a big screen. In the yard next to the building were two government-issue sedans and an open-cockpit Cessna, all painted a drab federal olive.

They headed into the recreation room, where a pair of teenage Indians were playing pocket billiards. Walsh spied a pay phone on the opposite wall and began to drag the Duke toward it, when the accountant said, ''Jack, I have to go to the can.''

With a sigh of impatience Walsh pulled the key to the cuffs from his pocket and unlocked the prisoner's wrist. The Duke disappeared through the rest room door as Walsh picked up the receiver and punched ''O.'' Only there wasn't any dial tone. He clicked the cradle several times, but still nothing. He turned helplessly toward the two kids at the pool table.

"Phone ain't worked for a couple days," one said.

"Okay," said Walsh, accustomed now to there being more flies than ointment, "so where do I make a call?"

The two Indians looked at each other neutrally and shrugged. "There's one in the bureau office," said the first one. "Only it's closed till Monday," his buddy added. And that was that. Walsh knew it would be useless to ask if there were any more phones in the village. A sense of unutterable weariness washed over him as he stared out the window at the shacks and old cars that dotted the interminable flatland. There just weren't going to be any breaks at all. He and the Duke would probably have to walk across New Mexico and Arizona.

As he jiggled the cuffs that dangled from his wrist, waiting for his prisoner, he heard a strange out-of-tempo engine sputter into life, very close and loud as a superpowered lawn mower. Half in a dream he turned to the sound and saw the Cessna swing away from the government cars toward the rear of the building. The part that was like a dream was Jonathan Mardukas, sitting in the open cockpit and looking like the Red Baron.

"Son of a bitch!" bawled Walsh, stomping his foot like a furious spoiled child. He pivoted like a basketball player and sprinted for the door. "Fear of flying, my ass!"

As he ran around the building, the Cessna was already taxiing toward the dusty landing strip. Slow and lumbering, it bumped across the prairie grass. The Duke looked over his shoulder and saw that Walsh was on his tail. The bounty hunter hadn't run so fast in a long, long time, his legs pumping in a double-time sprint. As he raced for the plane, one hand reaching out as if to grab its tail, he mentally closed the distance between them—Zen in the service of bloodlust.

The Duke had to negotiate a half turn in order to make a straight run on the landing strip. As he brought the plane around, the bounty hunter broke to the left and ran for the asphalt, knowing the Duke would have to pass that way. It just depended how fast. From the back doors of several shacks, Indians stepped out to see what was going on, as if with a sixth sense for a certain kind of trouble. By now the Cessna was bearing down the dusty runway, gathering speed as it rushed at Walsh. They were playing chicken again.

The bounty hunter could feel the wind from the looming propeller as he skipped and sidled out of harm's way. The plane trundled by, and he crouched and sprang, grabbing hold of the wing. He could feel the muscles rip in his armpits. He roared like a grizzly bear as he hooked a foot in the strut and hoisted himself alongside the cockpit. The Duke took his eyes off the landing strip and stared in astonished dismay at his sudden passenger.

"Get out of that plane!" screamed Walsh.

A noble light flooded the Duke's face. "My work is done here, Jack," he shouted back. "I've reopened the lines of communication between you and Gail and Denise. What more do you want?"

Walsh needed the extra bit of rage to clamber up to the edge of the cockpit. "I'm gonna open your fuckin' head!" he bellowed, grabbing at the accountant's shirt.

The plane was veering off the landing strip and bumping like crazy on the tufted grass, but the Duke was still in control. He slapped Walsh's hand away and continued his sanctimonious farewell. "*And* I think you're well on your way to reexamining who you are as a human being," he shouted, triumphant as an aria. Walsh made a lunge and gripped him around the shoulders, then started to drag him bodily out of the cockpit. The Duke yelped as the Cessna zigzagged wildly across the prairie. "You're going to get us killed!"

"I don't give a fuck!" shrieked Walsh, with truly Neanderthal ferocity. He was half inside the plane now, and the Duke was half out. No one was at the controls anymore, and the plane began to move in a wide arc, bouncing across the dry bed of a stream. The two men wrestled and tore at each other, till even the Duke couldn't think of a clever retort. Walsh struggled to pull an arm free and managed to right-hook the Duke on the chin, knocking him for a loop. As the Duke sagged against him, Walsh dropped away from the runaway plane, dragging his prisoner with him.

They landed in a heap in burrs and foxtails, finally shaking loose the accumulation of Texas dust. The Cessna continued its mad cavort across the flats, acting as if it meant to go overland to California, and generally looking as useless and ass-backwards as every other government vehicle. Walsh heaved the Duke to his feet. The wayward accountant was still reeling from both the punch and the fall, but even in his dazed state he seemed to know it was Walsh's turn. He stumbled along the dry wash as the bounty hunter shoved him.

"Let me tell you about the coffee shop I'm gonna open!" yelled Walsh, as if he still had to shout to be heard over the noise of the disappearing plane. "That's what I'm gonna do with my hundred grand! Maybe when you get out, if they don't kill you first, you can come pay me a visit!"

As they reached the far end of the landing strip and turned toward the settlement, they could see a pickup truck rattling in their direction, kicking up clouds of dust. It was the very truck that had brought them here, and the Indian who was driving—with the long black ponytail—seemed convinced he had brought a curse on his tribe. Walsh grabbed the Duke by the collar, and they waited till the pickup had skidded to a swerving halt beside them. The Indian leaped out with a warrior's fury.

"Man, what the hell are you *doin'?*" he demanded of Walsh. "You stole the Bureau plane. Are you crazy? Don't you think we don't got enough problems around here?"

The Duke opened his mouth to apologize, and Walsh yanked his collar to shut him up. Then the bounty hunter drew the .45 from his pocket and trained it on the Indian. "You just stay right there," he said. The Indian raised his hands slowly, betrayal and disappointment glinting in the jet of his eyes. Walsh tried not to see any of that. He hauled the Duke over to the pickup, yanked the door, and stuffed him in. Still holding the gun on the Indian, Walsh managed to cuff the Duke in the truck with one nimble hand.

He was not supposed to have this sinking feeling in his stomach. As he went around and got in the truck to drive away, he hated having to turn his eyes from the Indian silently staring in disbelief. It was all supposed to be simpler than this. He would not look in the rearview mirror as they drove away down the landing strip. Spare me the noble savage bit, he thought, swallowing a sour taste. And if the accountant had opened his mouth just then, no matter how small the remark, Jack Walsh would have happily blown his head away and kissed off the hundred grand.

They drove a hundred miles in silence, leaving the reservation and crossing the border into New Mexico, though the gray and ochre reaches of the landscape hadn't perceptibly changed. Nor had Walsh's mood, to judge by the scowl that hadn't left his face since they stole the truck. But the Duke had been doing his deep breathing exercises for the whole last hour, and he was serene and spunky again, ready to pick up the thread. "Jack, let's be fair about this," he observed, mild as a tribal elder. "You lied to me, too. At the river you promised to let me go."

Silence for a moment, as if Walsh were trying to resist the ongoing battle of wits that never seemed to get them anywhere but trouble. Finally his anger won out. "You lied to me first," he retorted.

"Yes, that's true. But the river was before you knew I'd lied to you, so that doesn't really count. You see what I mean?"

"Huh?" Somebody ought to put a meter on the Duke's mouth, so he couldn't say more than three words at a time.

"I mean, of course, it's wrong that I lied to you," the accountant continued, splitting hairs even further. "But you had no knowledge that I was lying about my aziophobia when we were in the river, which is when you lied to me."

Walsh laughed in spite of himself. You had to admire the guy's footwork. "I can't even argue with you, Jonathan," he said. "I don't know *what* you're talkin' about most of the time." Suddenly something twisted his features into a scowl again, and he grabbed his gut. "Ah, shit!" he moaned, as if a boring acquaintance had just dropped in.

The Duke leaned forward and peered in the bounty hunter's face. "I knew it, Jack. You've got an ulcer, don't you?"

"Yes, I've got an ulcer!" Walsh snapped irritably. He was *so* sick of traveling with a lay internist. "A big, fuckin' ulcer the size of a baseball! And all your bullshit is startin' to make it bleed again."

The Duke ignored the diatribe against himself. "We'd better get something to coat it with," he said.

There we go with that "we" stuff again, thought Walsh. It was *his* stomach and *his* ulcer, dammit. "I need somethin' to eat, that's all I need," he answered dismissively, pushing away the Duke's concern.

"But I can take care of that," the Duke declared with

calm and perfect confidence. All that deep breathing! "Now just take this exit."

And Walsh was too queasy to argue. They came off the road into a soulless town whose main excuse was three gas stations staring sullenly at one another at an intersection. A convenience store and a chain diner called Uncle Roy's made up the rest of the dead downtown, with a crisscross of railroad tracks and a depot just beyond. Decisively the Duke directed the bounty hunter into the diner's parking lot. "Now give me that FBI badge," he said to Walsh. The bounty hunter balked and scowled even deeper. "Listen, do you want to eat or not?"

Reluctantly he slipped the badge from his pocket and handed it over. Even *more* reluctantly he unlocked the cuffs and stowed them under the seat. Then, holding his belly gently, he followed his prisoner into the diner. The Duke was bristling with energy and authority as he approached the sparrowlike woman who stood at the register. "I want to speak to the manager immediately," he announced briskly, flashing the badge.

The woman stared at the brutal officiousness of the document, unnerved as an illiterate afraid she's going to be asked to read aloud. Her fear and distrust of cops were probably well earned. She excused herself with a murmur and called through a window into the kitchen, "Ped, you better get out here."

Wiping his hands on a greasy towel, a tough-looking dude stepped in from the kitchen, an impatient and paranoid "What now" look on his thick features. He had big, angry scars on either forearm, like someone who'd scraped off his own tattoos. "Yeah, what?" he said in a surly voice, which melted into honey as soon as he saw the badge.

"Alonso Mosely, FBI," declared the Duke imperiously. "My partner and I have been tracking a ring of counterfeiters who've been passing phony hundred-dollar bills throughout the state.'' Walsh could see the man called Ped visibly relax. Walsh had hauled in a hundred guys just like him, who'd been on probation ever since puberty. ''Tell me, have you received any hundreds in the last couple hours?''

''Yeah, yeah,'' retorted Ped enthusiastically, eager now to help and get them gone. '' 'Bout forty-five minutes ago somebody paid with a C-note.''

The Duke nodded gravely. ''Would you mind opening the register, please?'' Instantly the man slammed a button on the spring-drawer upright, whipping open the cash drawer. As he reached toward one of the compartments, the Duke protested, ''No, no! Don't touch it!'' Ped withdrew his hand as if he'd burned it on the stove. Elaborately the Duke took a paper napkin from a dispenser and reached in the cash drawer himself, extracting the suspicious bill. He laid it carefully on the counter, then snapped his fingers at the waitress. ''Pencil, please.''

Swiftly she raised a birdlike hand and drew a pencil from the tight bun of her hair. She handed it timidly to the Duke, who passed it to Walsh. ''Check that bill, Lieutenant.''

Walsh bent close to the greenback and made several small erasures along the border. Then he picked it up by the corners and held it to the light. He even smelled it. After each test he nodded at the Duke with a somberness worthy of *Dragnet*. ''Oh, yeah,'' he said at last, his brow creased with forensic concern, ''this one's bad.''

The manager looked at them curiously, as if taking them in for the first time. ''Gee, you guys look like you've been through the ringer.''

''Man, you don't know the half of it,'' Lieutenant Walsh replied, shaking his head and clucking his tongue.

The Duke's eyes darted from the man to the woman. ''I

want you to describe exactly what the person looked like who gave you this bill.''

''Well, he was a man,'' drawled the waitress, shy and uncertain, fearful of being punished if she said the wrong thing. '' 'Bout thirty. Tall.''

''Oh, yes, that's him,'' the Duke declared, sharing a knowing smile with the good lieutenant, who maintained an expression of beetle-browed seriousness. ''Listen, I want you to call all the other restaurants in the area and advise them of the situation. We're right behind him now, and I've got a very good feeling we'll have him in hand before the day is out.'' He plucked the bill from Walsh's hand, not taking much care about fingerprints. ''Evidence,'' he said with curt officiousness. Walsh could see an involuntary twinge of doubt pass across the manager's face. ''Lieutenant,'' said the Duke, ''make sure they get a receipt for this.''

The accountant slipped the money in his pocket and headed blithely out the door. Hurriedly Walsh scribbled with a pencil on the waitress's pad beside the register. He tore off the sheet and handed it to the manager. ''It's as good as gold,'' he declared with heart-wringing sincerity. ''You're a credit to your nation, sir. We'll be back. If you see anything suspicious, you just dial zero and ask for the FBI.''

Walsh bolted out into the street, afraid the Duke might have gotten away, but caught sight of him immediately in the convenience store across the way. As Walsh rushed in to join him he heard the melancholy whistle of a freight train in the distance. The Duke had already stuffed a cart with bananas and nuts and yogurt. He was drinking a quart of buttermilk out of the carton as Walsh dumped ready-made sandwiches and beer into the cart. The bounty hunter tore into a package of doughnuts and crammed them into his mouth two at a time.

They reached the counter and separated their clashing items into two stubborn piles. The Duke added cheese and Raisin Bran to his, and Walsh sprinted to the freezer for a brick of coffee ice cream. They were both nearly delirious with excitement, not having eaten a scrap since Ohio, and they greedily guarded their piles and insisted on separate bags. They'd blown fifty-four dollars of the hundred in thirty seconds flat. Walsh snatched the change from the cashier.

They came out of the store hugging their paper sacks to their chests. Down the street by the depot the engine of the freight train roared into view, and Walsh grinned with satisfaction as the line of boxcars began to trundle past. So maybe they'd got a *little* bit of a break. "C'mon, Jonathan," Walsh said merrily. "We're catchin' that train."

The Duke blanched as Walsh darted across to the pickup and reached in for the cuffs. As he trotted back, the accountant was shaking his head. "Yeah, I know, you can't do it," sneered Walsh. "You also couldn't fly. Now start running."

Cradling their priceless sacks of provision, the two men sprinted down the dispirited main street toward the depot. At the diner window the manager and his waitress peered in confusion. They hadn't liked the look of the dirt-caked pickup truck, but she told him that was "camelflage." Now they watched in dismay as the two agents began loping along the tracks, waiting for an open boxcar. The manager and the waitress had seen too many bums in their time. They exchanged a wilted look, then the manager strode to the phone and dialed zero. "Gimme the FBI," he said with a sort of hollow self-importance.

The freight train must have been two hundred cars long. Walsh and the Duke jogged along beside it, the big block-lettered railroad names looming by like moving billboards— Santa Fe, Erie Northern, Boston & Maine. At last a rust-red car trundled by with a wide open door. Walsh was trying to think quick how he could jump and drag the Duke with him in one fluid move, when suddenly the Duke tossed his bag of groceries into the boxcar and sprang up after it. As he hoisted himself through the doorway, Walsh stumbled over a rock.

He didn't exactly lose his footing, but the paper sack in his arms went flying. The Duke was leaning out of the boxcar watching. The sack burst open at Walsh's feet, sending doughnuts and sandwiches flying. It was one of those damned split-second decisions he had to make, because the boxcar was already ten feet away, and he knew he was getting winded. He couldn't stop to pick up so much as a can of beer as he ran to catch up. The Duke, sitting in the boxcar's doorway, was totally expressionless.

"Gimme your hand!" shouted Walsh as he came up level with the doorway.

The Duke's eyes gleamed, and his voice was very, very dry. "Do you promise to let me go?" Walsh was so shocked that he fell back three feet, and the Duke waved bye-bye. "See you in the next life, Jack!"

Nothing Walsh loved like a challenge. His face went red, and he gave out one of his Tarzan roars of stupefied rage. He felt a burst of speed like overdrive and ran neck and neck with the end of the boxcar, straining a hand to the iron ladder at the back. His fingers closed around one rung. He took the leap and hugged the ladder, his stomach tilting as he looked down at the rushing blur of the tracks. He forced himself to look up and stared into the shocked eyes of his prisoner, four feet away in the doorway. Walsh stretched out an arm and tensed to make the jump. The Duke pulled in like a turtle and slammed the door shut.

"You son of a bitch!" Walsh screamed, banging on the door with a fist. "You're gonna have to come out of there sometime, and I'll be waiting!" The train began to pick up speed as it left the jerkwater junction, and the wind against

Walsh's face was choked with dust. "You're only making it harder on yourself, Jonathan! I'm gonna break your knees if you leave me out here!"

Slowly the large door slid back on its iron track, revealing an angel-eyed Duke, smiling in a courtly way as he bowed the bounty hunter in. Walsh reached to the doorway and made the lunge, landing on his knees in the nearly empty boxcar. He was totally winded. The Duke was careful not to say anything clever, but walked across and sat on a stack of empty crates against the wall. At last, Walsh came to his feet, slapping the dust from his pants. Then he sauntered over to the Duke and kicked hard at the bottom crate, collapsing it and sending the Duke crashing on his ass.

"And don't you forget it!" snarled the bounty hunter. Then he headed down to the far end of the boxcar, as far away from the accountant as he could get, and slumped to the floor like a weary hunting dog. "I ain't talkin' to you for the rest of this trip," he announced with proud finality.

The Duke sighed heavily, as if he was dealing with a wayward child who wouldn't stop getting in trouble. "Now that's just adolescent," he said. "Don't you think, Jack? Two grown men can do better than that. All relationships have challenges, after all . . ."

Max Dorfler had been biting the inside of his lip for about two hours, ever since the Amarillo sheriff's men had released him from the wrecked car in the gorge. He was tired and dirty and nervous, sitting at a small table in a naked interrogation room. He was chain-smoking Marlboros, lighting one with the butt of another, trying to stay tough. He was getting very sick of local jails, and he longed to be back in L.A. so he could change hairpieces. The rug on his head was beginning to feel even to him like a veal cutlet.

The sheriff walked in, and Dorfler jumped to his feet. "Hey, are you guys gonna let me go or what? I'm tellin' ya, I don't know nothin'!"

The sheriff said nothing but stepped aside, and Mosely strode into the room, followed by his three stooges. "Is that a fact?" mocked the head agent with a grin. Dorfler suppressed a groan, but he didn't look tough anymore. "You just happen to be at the wrong place at the wrong time, is that it, Dorfler?"

Dorfler sat down on the chair in a gloomy funk. Mosely reached over and picked up Max's Marlboros where they sat beside the heaping ashtray. Mosely lit a cigarette, then pocketed the pack. "Where are they?" he asked, casually enough. Dorfler shrugged. Mosely kicked the chair out from under him, sending him tumbling to the floor. Agent Perry hurried forward and laid a restraining hand on the black man's arm, as if he was about to announce the rules of protocol. Savagely Mosely threw off the agent's hand. "Butt out," he growled.

He picked Dorfler up by the collar and shook him, the bounty hunter's head snapping back and forth like a spastic dummy. Then Mosely threw him at the table, which buckled and collapsed beneath the weight. As Dorfler hit the floor, Mosely went right down after him, pummeling with his fists. Even the sheriff, who loved nothing better than a lynching, seemed a bit nervous and murmured to Tuttle.

"I want some answers, and I want 'em now!" screamed Mosely. He grabbed the bounty hunter by the belt and the collar, picked him up bodily, and heaved him into a swivel chair, which skidded across the room like a Dodg'em car and slammed the wall. Dorfler looked very scared. Mosely started toward him with murderous single-mindedness, while the sheriff and the other agents tried to look at the floor.

"I don't know nothing, I tell ya!" Dorfler pleaded, shivering as if he would wet his pants at any moment.

"They went down the river. They're probably dead by now."

A deputy entered the room and whispered to Agent Plumides. Mosely turned at the interruption, and all his agents saw something disconnected and off-center in his blazing eyes. They squirmed uncomfortably. Plumides approached the chief in a sort of flinch, as if he expected that Mosely might deck him, as well. "Sir," he murmured, taking care not to lock eyes with the black man, "it seems that an Agent Mosely and his partner were seen hopping a westbound freight near Channing."

Silence for a moment. Nobody made a move, waiting to see what Mosely would do. Dorfler's eyes were fixed on his hairpiece in the corner. The sheriff's mind was racing, trying to construct an alibi that put him somewhere else but here this afternoon. The glazed look in Mosely's eyes seemed to clear a little, but when he walked abruptly out of the room he was still in a kind of trance. Possessed. And though the three subagents hurried out after him like lemmings off a cliff, they didn't look happy at all. Perhaps they didn't believe anymore there was somebody out there computing their overtime.

10

HIS WHOLE BODY clenched against the cold, Jack Walsh huddled in a sort of yogi contortion against the wall of the boxcar. The night wind blew in through a hundred chinks. He actually had a headache from his teeth chattering so hard. But all of this was bearable so long as the Duke was at the opposite end of the car and quiet. It was too dark for them to see each other, and the battering noise of the train was a peaceful screen between them. For all his shivering, Walsh felt like a kid who'd waited his whole life for a room of his own.

Then came the voice, just a few feet away. "C'mon, Jack, don't be a baby. Are you going to sulk the rest of the trip?"

Walsh huddled even more, till he looked like a hedge-hog. It made him crazy to hear the Duke call it a trip, as if they were on their summer vacation. The constant picking and nagging was worse than being married to all of his sisters-in-law combined. The Duke crouched beside him, chin propped on the heel of his palm as he waxed philosophical. "You want to know when I knew I had you pegged?" he asked. Walsh could almost feel him smiling dreamily, and groaned to think they'd been together long

enough to be talking about the good old days when they
first met.

"The very first second we were in the car in New
York," continued the accountant fondly. "For some reason I noticed your watch. An old Timex." He snorted a
brief ironic laugh, curdled with sentimentality. "All
scratched and cracked—but you hung onto it, didn't you?
Even when you could've gotten a brand new digital for ten
bucks."

Walsh unclenched from the hedgehog position and slowly
sat up. Now they were sitting side by side, scarcely a foot
between them. It was still ridiculously cold, though the
bounty hunter's teeth had stopped chattering. Enough of
the moonlight spilled through the chinks in the rusty car
that they could have seen each other's faces, but for the
present both of them stared carefully ahead.

"Let me guess," said the Duke. "It was a present,
right? Someone gave it to you, must be twenty years ago
by now." Seventeen, thought Walsh, but he said nothing.
Yet imperceptibly he tilted his wrist in his lap and made
out the dim, luminous dial. "So I knew you were sentimental. Memories are precious to you. It's been my expe-
rience that sentimental people have a desire to do what's
right. I knew you wouldn't force me to fly, Jack."

Walsh brought the Timex close to his face, not caring
that the Duke was watching. Even in this bitter cold there
was no mist in the crystal. A better watch was never made.
"Gail," he said, though the point was obvious enough by
now. "It was the first thing she ever got me. 'Cause I was
always a half hour late when we were dating."

He made a helpless grab at the air with his other hand.
Jesus, if he could just turn the little sucker back a few
years. All those good times happened once. Didn't that
make them permanent, sort of? "When she bought it she
set it a half hour fast," he said, "so I'd always be on

time.'' The Duke chuckled appreciatively, and Walsh, suddenly shy, tucked his wrists between his legs before the accountant could see he was still on Gail's time.

He rolled his head to the side and looked through a chink at the moon. ''Somewhere in the back of my mind,'' he said, so softly the Duke wasn't meant to hear, ''I still imagine we're gonna end up together. I'm still waiting, ya know? Hangin' on.''

The Duke missed nothing. ''I don't think she's coming back,'' he said in a neutral voice. There wasn't a trace of judgment or disdain.

Walsh was quiet for a long moment. The moon disappeared from the chink, having risen a little or set a little. Astronomy wasn't the bounty hunter's strong suit. ''I don't, either,'' he said at last, flashing a mournful grin in the dark. He paused as if to let the Duke say more, but nothing came. The accounting part was over with. ''The bitch,'' said Walsh, with an awful lack of conviction.

Once more Dorfler's belongings were spilled out of a brittle manila envelope on the table before him. He could practically hear Walsh laughing at him. A shredded, filter-torn cigarette was the last thing to roll from the envelope. ''The fed took my cigarettes,'' Dorfler said to the sergeant, who passed him a release form to sign.

''Lousy habit,'' the sergeant replied indifferently.

''Took my lighter, too,'' continued the bounty hunter, a whine creeping into his voice.

''Yeah, well, what do you expect from the feds? I guess you'll have to catch up with 'em in Flagstaff. If you ask me, it's cheaper to quit.''

Dorfler's ears perked at the name. He didn't seem whiny at all as he shoved his stuff in his pockets and sprinted out of the Amarillo station, bound for Arizona.

• • •

Walsh crouched in the open doorway of the boxcar, most of his weight on one leg, and dragged on a Camel as he watched the dawn. Though he usually loved the special chill of early morning and the rose and gold of the rising sun, he was too raw and ashen from a bumpy night to care much. He hadn't heard the Duke's voice in several hours, though neither of them had slept. Now the Duke tapped his shoulder and spoke with elaborate courtesy. "Jack, would you care to have breakfast with me?"

Walsh looked down at the gray blur of gravel beneath the train. He took a last pull on the cigarette butt, sucking it down low enough to burn his fingers. Then he cocked them and shot it away in the wind, like a firefly disappearing into the cauldron of the sun. He turned to see the Duke tear open the paper sack and set it down on the floor for a place mat. Methodically he laid out an orange and banana, a box of high-fiber cereal, a pint of nonfat milk.

He grinned brightly at Walsh and held out a couple of packaged cakes. "I think these are yours, anyway, Jack," he said. "*I* didn't buy any Ho-Hos and Suzy-Qs."

Walsh winced ever so slightly when he saw the Duke's face in the light. The accountant's jaw was puffy and bruised purple. "I'm sorry I hit you," said the bounty hunter.

The Duke shrugged, then beckoned Walsh to sit down. He waited till Walsh had torn open his Ho-Hos before starting to peel the orange. "Do you know where we are?"

"We've been going west all night," said Walsh, mumbling through his cake. "My guess is somewhere in Arizona. We're almost home."

"And I'm almost dead," the Duke observed laconically, pursing his lips as he chomped on his orange. He passed the carton of milk to Walsh and nodded for him to drink.

"Listen, the witness protection program ain't so bad."

Walsh swallowed the lump of cake and took a sip from the carton, just a sip. Then he placed it back next to the Duke's cereal. "They'll give you a new name. You'll have a whole new life."

The Duke sighed, and his voice was clipped. "Jack, do me a favor, okay? Don't play this big brother routine with me, because it really insults my intelligence. The only thing that's important to you about me is getting your money." There was an edge of dismissal in his tone that was absolutely ducal. With his thumbnail he carefully scored his cereal box so he could use it as a bowl.

Walsh slapped his Suzy-Qs on the floor. "Listen, I'm tired of you making me out to be some kinda thug who's out for a big hunk of change. Serano's guys offered me a million bucks for you, did ya know that?"

The Duke laughed curtly and poured his milk. "Hey, why not just go for the big money, Jack? You're doing his work for him either way." It wasn't the same, and the Duke knew it, but they hadn't had a good fight since Ohio.

"You don't know what you're talkin' about! The reason I *do* this shit is because I didn't want to work for that lowlife." The Duke munched his fiber and listened. He'd been waiting for Walsh to blow like this ever since he saw his wife and daughter. "You remember that dealer I was trying to bring down in Chicago? That was Serano, all right? Now you know everything. Are you happy, Jonathan?" Though he'd started out enraged and shrill, a pleading hurt had crept into his voice by the end, like an animal dragging around a broken foot.

"*He's* the reason you left Chicago? And now you're taking me in?" The Duke was genuinely shocked and thrown off-balance. For a man who had figured out Gail and Denise to a T, he couldn't believe he hadn't put two and two together. Then he was pissed. "Are you out of your mind? You want me to speak your language, Jack?

You let that mother-fucker *beat* you!'' He pounced on the word "mother-fucker" with more venom than he thought he had in him. To his own surprise, he liked the taste of the word in his mouth.

"Don't you see?" he continued passionately. "With what you know about police work and what I know about Serano's books, we could put him away for thirty years!"

Walsh squirmed slightly and squinted out at the rising sun, which had lost its rosy gilt and was just another day now. "I'm not in that business anymore," he said evenly.

"Look, all I am is a putz accountant, and *I* tried to get him. What's *your* excuse? You're this macho dude with a chip on your shoulder. You've got a gun and a load of bullshit from here to Texas, and all you really know how to do is back away." With a growl of disgust, the Duke went back to his cereal, shoveling it into his mouth with grim determination.

Walsh looked down and rubbed the face of his Timex. He seemed to have forgotten the fact that the Duke made him mad with his constant opinions. Of course, it was all his own fault that the Duke had backed him into a corner like this. When he was in his prime, nobody ever cornered Jack Walsh or ever got the drop on him. But that was then. "I just don't have it in me," he said simply.

"You're a coward, Jack. Why don't we just leave it at that."

Walsh glanced at the Duke with a kind of awe. Where had all this fierce and noble pride come from? For days now, Walsh's ace in the hole was his certainty that the Duke was ridiculous. A sweet guy and harmless, but totally absurd. Since when had he started to act like the Lone Ranger? For the first time Walsh understood how a mouse could bring down a lion's empire. It stung him with inadequacy, but curiously he felt no anger at all at the Duke's abusive words. Envy perhaps, but no anger.

There was a catch in the train's rhythm, and in a flash the bounty hunter was on his feet, leaning out of the boxcar. A couple of miles up ahead he could see the straggling outskirts of a city. Walsh could see they were high on a mountain plain, banked with a forest of cedar and pine, but he hadn't a clue what the city was. The course of his hunter's life was New York/Chicago/L.A., with the occasional side to Vegas. This was the moon to him.

He turned and barked at the Duke, "C'mon, we're gettin' off here. Just in case."

The Duke was right beside him, watching the rushing ground outside, waiting for the exact moment. It was as if they had more serious things to argue about than jumping off trains, or perhaps the teamwork had become second nature. Walsh gave him the first grin. "You first, wise guy," he said, and the Duke made a leap like a paratrooper. Walsh jumped blindly after him—as usual, not figuring out a landing strategy till the ground was in his face.

Four minutes later, punctually on schedule, the 6:04 from Santa Fe rolled into the Flagstaff station. It had scarcely rolled to a halt when a swarm of men—feds and cops together, manic as a posse—started rolling the doors of the boxcars open, shining torches and yelling orders. Indeed it was a tribute to the Bonnie-and-Clyde maneuvering of the bounty hunter and his prey that the ranks of those pursuing them had grown to be an army.

When the manhunt was in full cry, an unmarked black Lincoln came speeding into the depot. It rocketed to a stop about halfway along the snaking trail of boxcars. Mosely jumped out, followed by his scrambling trio of subs. The black man approached a police captain who stood by the tracks with walkie-talkies in either hand. Mosely raised his eyebrows by way of greeting, and the captain shook his head. "Not yet."

Mosely could see that the wave of cops had opened the train like a can of sardines all the way back to the caboose. Perry, ever the least timid of the subs, stepped up beside him and said, "Sir, they could have jumped off the train anywhere along the line."

The black man shook his head with an air of assurance that was most impressive, given the bungling of the last few days. "Walsh isn't playing with a lot of time," he replied. "He took this train as far as he could. He's around here somewhere."

He wasn't the only one who thought so. A rental car of painfully modest proportions cruised the parking lot by the station, modest at least compared to the Caddies a man like Dorfler was used to. The second-string bounty hunter could see in a flash that the search was proving fruitless. He didn't even stop to make certain, but did a quick U-turn and headed for the outskirts. He was so primed for finding Walsh he could practically smell him.

By now Walsh and the Duke had trotted through the railroad fields to the first outposts of commerce, a strip of linoleum merchants and massage parlors cheek by jowl with the Colonel and Ronald McDonald. Walsh pointed to the half-acre lot of a chain grocery, and the Duke followed dutifully as the bounty hunter eyeballed various vehicles. Walsh pointed down the line at the row of Arizona license plates.

"Do I know my shit or what?" he said proudly, making a beeline toward a black Jeep CJ-7, obviously brand new. It hardly looked like an off-road vehicle, accoutered more to impress the kids in a college town. Walsh beckoned the Duke around to the doorless driver's side. He centered the Duke's shoulders to make the widest possible shield, then took a last quick look around. He crawled in on the front seat, rolled over on his back, and dropped to the floor. He squinted in concentration as he felt for the wires under the dash.

The Duke shot nervous glances toward every customer who exited the store, fearing the owner would return. But it was barely thirty seconds before he heard the satisfying thrill of a well-tended engine as it hot-wired to life. Walsh grinned up at him, and the Duke rushed around to the passenger's side, feeling more conspicuous than ever. Yet he couldn't help but be stirred by Walsh's sense of exhilaration, even as Walsh cuffed him to the roll bar.

Walsh peeled out, laughing like a kid on a joy ride. As they passed the front of the grocery store, a couple of cheery coeds came jaunting out and froze in disbelief at their disappearing wheels. The Duke managed to give them a sympathetic shrug, even with his arm stretched up to the roll bar. And then they were speeding away, leaving the commercial strip behind and heading for fields and mountains.

"Where are we going *now?*" asked the Duke.

"To the next airport!" Walsh replied with enthusiasm, drinking in the mountain air in great gulps and reaching for a cigarette. But the moment of intoxication was very short-lived, for he looked in the rearview mirror and saw a cop car coming up fast behind them. "Oh, shit!" groaned the bounty hunter, as the cop car hit its lights and siren.

Walsh stomped on the gas pedal, and the huge tires squealed beneath them like a terrified rabbit. The bracing air filled with the stink of burned rubber. Then Walsh groaned again as he peered over the steering wheel to make sure he was seeing right. There was a squad car coming toward them from the opposite direction, and he and the Duke were about to be the bologna in the sandwich. Walsh pounded the steering wheel with both hands like a tom-tom, screaming with fury.

The Duke railed at him. "You're not going to be happy till you get us both killed, are you?"

"I've come too far!" bellowed the bounty hunter. "I'm too close!"

The cop car ahead slammed on its brakes and skidded to a stop with a sharp fishtail, blocking the road before them. When the Duke realized Walsh wasn't going to stop he started to scream—"Nooooo!"—in one long, banshee syllable. His hands flew up to cover his eyes, just as Walsh jerked the wheel to the right. The Jeep lurched up a low embankment to the road's shoulder, kicking up chunks of earth. By the time the dirt clods had exploded on the windshield of the sideways cop car, the Jeep had already passed around the barricade. The squad car speeding in their wake tried the same maneuver. But as it started onto the shoulder it shaved away the grill and headlights of the stationary car and spun to an ignominious halt.

As Walsh crowed in the fleeing Jeep, the defeated cops reached painfully for their radio mikes. The only way that Walsh could tell they were heading west was from the angle of the sun behind them. The wind that buffeted them through the open sides of the Jeep made it impossible for the Duke to talk, which was a blessing. Then Walsh looked in the rearview mirror again, and this time there were a half dozen cop cars roaring after them like a school of killer sharks.

"How many fuckin' cops can they have in this town?" yelled the bounty hunter. And at that the Duke poked his shoulder and pointed right. Heading their way down a dirt road that short-cut from the train depot was a line of flashing cars, local and feds together. With a sinking feeling Walsh looked left, and from that direction too the jaws of the law were speeding toward them. It was a goddamned convention.

As Walsh sped through the intersection of the dirt roads,

he could feel all the cop cars gathering on his tail in a tidal wave of convergence. The sirens and blazing lights were a regular Mardi Gras parade. Now, looming ahead, was the worst sight yet: a phalanx of federal cars standing in the road like a line of chariots. Ten men in blue suits flanked the cars in wide stances of combat readiness. The Duke reached over and gripped Walsh's arm. "I know you can do it, Jack!" he shouted.

Do what, thought the bounty hunter, even as he whipped the steering wheel to hard right. The Jeep crashed through a prairie fence of rotted wood slats and chicken wire. Walsh yanked the shift into four-wheel drive as they bounced across a broad sunny field, the chicken wire on the grill like the net on a widow's hat. Immediately a wave of cop cars swerved off the road in pursuit. But the very first one, a local Flagstaff black-and-white, had hardly thudded fifty feet into the field before it wrenched against a rock and snapped its axle. It was maddeningly apparent that none of the flashing, blaring vehicles was capable of a chase across open country.

But the chopper was. As the black Jeep sailed up a meadowed hill of mountain daisies, slaloming around stands of aspen, the helicopter loomed hungrily in hot pursuit. Mosely was next to the pilot, his eager, predatory body hunched forward in the bubble. The three subagents sat crunched together in the back, all their shoulders pulled up to their ears. The Jeep had almost reached the crest of the hill. Mosely barked at the pilot, "Check the other side!"

Back on the road, where three dozen cop cars huddled in impotent rage, Max Dorfler cruised by in his rental Fiesta. He knew he didn't stand a chance of following the Jeep, but he noted the chopper as it banked away over the hill, and he saw the trace of a dirt road in the meadow below. He gunned his pathetic, one-horse engine and crossed his fingers that the dirt track would feed its way down to the main road.

When the Jeep cleared the crest of the ridge the Duke could feel his stomach drop to his ankles, a horrible *déjà vu* of the moment the day before when they'd gone through the bridge rail into the gorge. The Jeep was built to land pretty easily, but the slope this side was very steep. They tore down the hill at nightmare speed, Walsh's hands helpless on the wheel. Where the slope flattened out below was a cluster of Norman Rockwell farmhouses, with wide sun-splotched meadows beyond. A horseshoe grove of conifers wrapped around and through the dusty red barns and silos.

The accountant screamed, raising both knees to his chest and clenching his eyes shut, as if this could protect him from the razorback hunk of granite that jutted out from the bleached grass of the hillside. The Jeep raked over the rock, which tore its underbelly and dragged its speed in half. It zigzagged left and headed straight for a lonesome pine. There was nothing left of the steering as it slammed the tree sideways, stopped dead in its tracks. The only reason the Duke wasn't thrown was his being cuffed to the roll bar, and Walsh stayed on because he'd clutched the accountant like a teddy bear the moment he saw the tree.

No broken bones. By now they were used to being bruised and shaken. Walsh drew the key from his pocket and uncuffed the Duke. They tumbled out of the Jeep and started running toward the farmhouses. The chopper was on them like a magnet, Mosely leaning out as it dropped below the treeline and chased the scurrying pair. As the wind from the chopper stirred the grass like a storm at sea, Walsh and the Duke headed into a field of winter wheat and hit the dirt. The chopper zoomed over and swooped above the silos, banking to turn about.

Walsh and the Duke skittered through the grass on

hands and knees, as if they'd dropped a rung on the scale of evolution. By the time the chopper passed over the waving field again, the two men had reached a thicket of low trees. They kept beneath the overhang of branches and made their way to the side of the dirt road. They could hear the chopper, angry as a hornet, cruising low among the farm buildings. They ducked as a couple of federal sedans roared past on the dirt road, followed by two local black-and-whites.

All the activity seemed to be focused among the farmhouses, from which the good hill folk were pouring in bewilderment and dismay. Walsh spotted another car coming along the dirt road, and this time it had no lights on top. It was also moving much slower than all the cop cars. "I believe this is our cab," said the bounty hunter, nudging the Duke to step onto the road with him. Walsh felt as though he was about to rob a stagecoach. He was relieved to see there was only the driver in the car. It was about time, he thought, for a little luck to fall their way.

He yanked out his .45 and waved a slow arm to flag down the car. As it pulled closer it began to slow, a flashy little white Fiesta. Walsh walked toward it, brandishing his gun in one hand and his FBI badge in the other. He was working so hard to look like a cop, despite his bum's appearance, that he didn't really pay attention to the curious feeling of something familiar. The sun was glinting off the windshield, so he couldn't really see the driver's face.

"Jack, don't!" cried the Duke. "It's Dorfler."

Walsh stopped like a deer dazed by headlights. The Fiesta gunned toward him. Walsh spun around and started to lunge away, and he would've made it if Dorfler hadn't opened the door. Which crashed into the bounty hunter and threw him sprawling in the dirt. The Duke looked aghast at the sight of his captor's inert body, and he ran for the grove of aspens on the far side of the road.

Dorfler bolted out of his car, completely uninterested in the groaning form of his fellow bounty hunter. He tore after the Duke, darting through the glittering trees as they quaked in the mountain breeze. The Duke was in better condition and had better reflexes, so he stayed fifty feet ahead, sliding down an embankment and splashing through a creek. He danced from rock to rock and had already made it to the other side before Dorfler reached the stream. The Duke might really have gotten away if it hadn't been for his bloody good nature.

But he stopped and started to think about Walsh. He hesitated, turned around, blinked at the flash of the sun on the stream. And suddenly Dorfler was on the opposite bank, pointing a gun at his head. The accountant froze, relieved in a way to have it all decided for him. Dorfler splashed across the stream toward him, and the Duke held up his hands for the cuffs. Dorfler threw a punch and smashed the accountant's jaw—the opposite jaw from the one that Walsh had smashed in the Cessna.

As the accountant reeled, Dorfler dragged him bodily through the stream and up the embankment. He kept pummeling the Duke and slamming his head. They came out of the grove of aspens. Beside the Fiesta, Walsh was on his hands and knees, trying to get the cobwebs out of his head. From his knee to his hip was a mind-numbing pain where the door of the car had slammed him. Dorfler hauled the Duke over to the car, snapped open the trunk, and dumped the prisoner in. As he slammed the trunk closed, Walsh was tottering to his feet.

Dorfler came around the side of the car, and Walsh took a feeble swing at him, nearly falling over in the process. Dorfler obliged him with another left hook, stumbling him backwards, then pounding Walsh's gut like a punching bag till he crashed to the ground among the aspens.

Dorfler raced to his car and did a swift three-point turn in the dirt, heading back over the ridge toward Flagstaff. By the time Walsh came to, the squad of cop cars had given up the chase among the farmhouses and roared away, unaware of Dorfler's flank maneuver. Walsh blinked his eyes open in time to see the reluctant chopper overhead as it made a final pass on its homeward flight. But for the longest time, Walsh didn't do anything but stare up at the shivering leaves of an aspen. The sweet smell of leaf mold was all around him, and he could hear the babble of the stream below the embankment. For a while there, he was sure he had died and gone to heaven.

It was sunset by the time Walsh reached the end of the dirt road. At the intersection with pavement sat a rattletrap one-room diner with an "EAT" sign on a creaking hinge. He looked around automatically, but for once nobody appeared to be staking him out. He headed through the screen door that sported a tin ad for "Orange Crush." At the counter was a middle-aged woman with an ample bosom and a matronly bun of hair. She kneaded the small of her back with her fingertips. She didn't blink twice at Walsh's ragged appearance. She was apparently quite accustomed to men at the end of their rope.

"Bad day?" she asked sympathetically as he hobbled to one of the counter stools.

"Bad week," he replied ruefully. She liked that. A deep whiskey laugh percolated in her throat. He gave her the bruised remnant of a grin. "I could use a cup of coffee."

"Then you came to the right place, honey," she said. In a second she'd slid a heavy tan mug of coffee under his nose, dragging over the cream and sugar. She watched

Walsh for a moment as he stirred it all together, then
disappeared through the swing door into the kitchen, as if
she wanted to give him a little breathing room.

Walsh put his elbows on the Formica, his head in his
hands. Twisting his wrists, he rubbed deeply into his eye
sockets, trying to smooth out the tight cap of pain that
hooded over his eyes. He heard a delicate sliding noise
coming toward him along the counter. He took one knuckle
out of his eye and glanced down, just in time to see
Mosely's military shades bump up against his coffee mug.
Carefully Walsh picked up the mug and took a slurp of
coffee.

He didn't look toward the far end of the counter, though
he could feel the black man's stare crawling up and down
his spine. Walsh took another gulp of coffee, figuring it
might be a long stretch before he had another glimmer of
home cooking. Then he picked up the glasses and propped
them on his nose. "Well, what do you know," he said.
"I've been lookin' all over for these."

The Flagstaff airport was hanky-sized, served by a couple of modest, short-run airlines that were a miracle of
deregulation. Dorfler pulled into the terminal parking lot,
where a chain link fence stretched and buckled and sagged
around a field the size of a playground and a single
runway. Dorfler had noticed the Duke was acting a little
spacy, but now the accountant's knees began to twitch
with nerves. He made a sound that was something between
a whimper and a cleared throat.

"Excuse me," said the Duke in a small voice, "I can't
do this. I have a very serious fear of flying."

He gave Dorfler a wincing look, flushing apologetically.
Dorfler nodded gravely, seeming to brood over the psy-
chological complications. He looked out the window at the
row of single-engine aircraft lined up by the chain link

fence. Then he looked back at the Duke, who shrugged at the stupid irony of it all. Then, in one smooth, unbroken stroke, the bounty hunter brought up his fist and crashed it into the side of the Duke's head. The accountant slumped unconscious against the door.

The all-purpose Dorfler cure.

Jack Walsh sat in a stiff-backed chair in the tiny interrogation cubicle, his legs crossed and his arms folded over his chest. A Camel dangled smoldering from his lips, squinting his eyes till they were like slits. He flicked his wrist and glanced at the Timex. Quarter to seven.

"Forget about your time clock, Walsh," growled Mosely. "It's over. Kiss it good-bye."

Perry, Tuttle, and Plumides stood like a mute choir behind their chief, as tightly packed in the tiny room as they'd been in the chopper. They mimicked the black man's smirk of superiority exactly.

"I know my rights," said Walsh, sounding exceedingly bored. "You owe me some phone calls."

Mosely stooped and spat the next words in his face. "What you should worry about right now, asshole, is the ten years you're going to get for impersonating a federal agent."

Walsh's eyebrows shot up in surprise. "Ten years, huh? How come nobody's after you?"

Mosely's eyes smoldered. "You don't know when to quit, do you?" There was almost a tinge of pity in the agent's voice, but it could have been self-defeat. The three subagents shifted uneasily. They hadn't won a round in so long, they couldn't even remember what it felt like. Each of them longed to pull out his badge to prove he was still there at all.

"I just know one thing," Walsh said through a shroud

of smoke. "By law, you guys owe me phone calls. And I ain't sayin' shit till I get 'em."

Some laws Mosely would have laid his life on the line for. Some he would have sacrificed all three of his sub-agents to enforce. The phone law was not one of them. Just now the phone law seemed like a communist plot that would one day threaten the freedom of all good men. Mosely turned and rolled his bitter eyes at his trusty team. "Give him his fuckin' calls," he said wearily to Tuttle.

Walsh spat the butt of his Camel on the floor. As Tuttle led him out to the booking room, the bounty hunter began to whistle, *Reach out and touch someone* . . . Mosely looked as if the Russian flag had just gone up at the Pentagon.

Jerry Geisler was a wreck. For days now his life had been a nightmare of paranoia. Every time he left Moscone's office he darted nervous looks up and down Vignes Street, watching for the battered van or, worse, Serano's guys. Tony Daruvo had told him bluntly over the phone that Jerry's ass was in a sling if he gave them any more bogus tips. "A minor attitude adjustment" was the way Tony put it, suave as always.

Now Jerry listened in a frenzy of nerves, clutching the extension to his ear as Moscone bawled at Walsh from the inner office. "I hope you're gettin' close, Jack," shrilled Moscone, "cause you only got five fuckin' hours!"

Walsh's voice was maddeningly dispassionate. "No, I'm not, Eddie," he purred. "I was just callin' to let you know you're a dead man. 'Cause you put Dorfler on this thing again . . . you lying scumbag."

You could hardly blame poor Eddie Moscone for losing it. He had everything riding on the Duke, and he was practically in a sugar coma from so many doughnuts. "I should kill *you*, you stupid son of a bitch!" he screamed into the mouthpiece. "You had the guy five days ago! What the hell are you joyridin' around the country for?" He stomped around his office, rattling the partitions like a 7.5 quake. "And are you *nuts*, tellin' Dorfler you were gettin' a hundred when I offered him twenty-five? He just calls me up yellin' and screamin'. What *I* wanna know is, why can't somebody get the bastard here before midnight?"

The whole bungalow was shaking now, and Jerry was getting the full force of it in stereo. He had to listen very hard to hear Walsh's soft and bewildered question when Eddie Moscone finally stopped to take a breath. "When did you speak to Dorfler?" the bounty hunter asked.

"Five minutes ago," barked Moscone. "What difference does it make?"

In Flagstaff there was a sudden look of marvelous surmise on Walsh's face. He didn't hear anything more that Moscone said, for he slowly lowered the phone in the cradle, staring intently across the booking room at a digital clock on the wall that read 7:03. But Walsh wasn't really looking at the time, short as it was. He gazed in the middle distance thinking, a crease folding the line between his eyebrows. Tuttle, who stood nearby, patiently waited for him to make his second call. Tuttle didn't care how long it took, since he was on over-overtime.

It was a long shot, ridiculously long, but Walsh dug out his wallet and retrieved the business card Tony Daruvo had given him at JFK. The numbers on the back had faded and run from the trip down the rapids, but Walsh could still read it. He punched in the number with a bitter half grin, never very good at playing games with million-to-one odds. A male voice answered, "Yeah?"

"Yeah," Walsh repeated, slow and quiet. He made his voice as blank as he could. "Is Tony or Joey there?"

"Who's this?" The voice was leary and pugnacious.

Walsh held his breath, and the odds shot up to *ten*

million to one. "Dorfler," he replied, with a top spin on the word that gave it a subtle, passive whine. Instantly Walsh could feel the guy on the other end relax.

"Sure, Max, hang on. I'll put you through."

A click and a small cascade of beeps. In a lower-floor hotel room in Vegas, with flocked walls and a ceiling mirror, Joey Ribuffo was reading the funnies with a perplexed frown when the phone rang. Instantly Joey picked it up. "Max?"

"No, it's Walsh," announced the gloating voice through the static. "So Dorfler's workin' for you guys now. Ain't that cozy?"

Joey didn't appear surprised or troubled in the least. "What're *you* complainin' for?" he asked. "We came to you first."

The toilet flushed in the bathroom, and Tony Daruvo came out, frowning at his nails and deciding he needed a manicure. Joey held out the phone and said with a snicker, "Walsh." Tony Daruvo's nostrils flared like a bull as he blurted grandly into the receiver, "Hey, too late, dickhead."

"No, Tony, too late for you," retorted Walsh, with a bravado that was impressive, considering he was in FBI custody six hundred miles away. "I didn't come this far not to collect my money. I want the Duke back."

"Oh, yeah? So what are you telling *me* for?"

"What am I telling you for, Tony? Because I got some of the Duke's belongings, that's why." Walsh chuckled softly through the phone, pausing for effect until a beat before he knew Tony would have to ask what. "Including a buncha computer disks," he went on finally, sharply enunciating every word, "of Serano's businesses and money-laundering operations. *And,* if I don't get him back in the next two hours I'm gonna turn it all over to the feds."

Tony's face began to twitch. "I'll blow your brains out, Walsh."

"Oh, really, Tony? And how you gonna do that from jail?" Tony didn't answer. He knew there was a deal about to come. He started to bite his thumbnail. "You tell Jimmy Serano I wanna meet him, *with* the Duke, *alone*. In two hours, in the main terminal at McCarran. That's where we'll make the exchange. If I see one single goon within a mile of that airport, the deal's off and I go to the feds."

Tony had already bitten two nails to the nub, but his voice was the same old cocky sneer. "I ain't gonna tell him that, Walsh. Screw you."

"Fine, Tony. After he's busted, I'll make sure to tell him you knew about it beforehand." Tony swallowed with difficulty. The sneer wilted on his lips. "That's two hours from now. Main terminal, McCarran Airport. You got that, moron? Have a nice day."

As soon as he plopped the phone in the cradle, Walsh shifted to a gear that was precise and economical as a laser. He had a lot to do in a very little time. His eyes fell distractedly on Tuttle, as he went over strategy in his mind. Tuttle squirmed and looked at the floor, wishing he had his two subpartners with him. He was afraid the prisoner was going to ask him something he didn't have the authority to answer.

"Tell Mosely I wanna make a deal," said Walsh, slouching against the wall by the phone.

"Inspector!" Tuttle bawled into the interrogation room, as if Walsh were picking on him. Immediately the black man appeared, Plumides and Perry in tow. Tuttle drew back with the other subs so the chief could have some privacy with the bounty hunter. When Mosely and Walsh were face to face, they were exactly the same height. "What would you do if I could deliver you Serano?" asked the bounty hunter.

Mosely shifted all his weight to one leg and crossed his arms over his chest. "How do you mean deliver?"

"For starters, conspiracy to destroy government evidence."

Mosely visibly tensed. "What government evidence would that be?"

Walsh shook his head, as if to say they were getting it out of order. "You'll have to let me take in the Duke myself, so I can collect my money."

Mosely was stunned to see that Walsh was serious. His air of toughness was wearing very thin. "Yeah, well, like I said, what evidence?"

Walsh grinned. "Alonso, my friend," he said, "I'll have to tell you on the way, because we gotta be in Vegas in two hours."

It was the name of the motel—*Golden Boy*—that convinced Dorfler to pull in and register, because otherwise it looked like every other bleached-out sleaze joint on the outer rims of Vegas. Dorfler was positive that the name foretold his glittering future, and thinking positive was always the key. The raft of books he'd read about success was about to pay off. None of which surprised Max Dorfler: he'd always known he'd be driving the bus someday, giving the orders.

He yanked the Duke's handcuffed wrist closer to the pipe under the bathroom sink. The accountant grunted and bit his bottom lip. Ever since Dorfler had taken him in Flagstaff he'd tried to tough it out, the way Jack Walsh would have done, so as not to let Dorfler see he'd had any effect. The bounty hunter slapped the other cuff around the pipe; it jangled with the sharp cold sound of metal on hollow metal.

"Now hold this up!" Dorfler ordered, whacking a folded newspaper across the accountant's face. With his one good hand the Duke tried to angle the paper toward the Polaroid camera Dorfler was pointing at him. The bounty hunter sighed with exasperation and straightened the paper so the headline was boldly prominent. "They gotta see it's today's date," he explained with exaggerated patience. "I got this all figured out. Now say 'cheese.' "

Dorfler started snapping off pictures, laying them out on the sink to develop. "Don't do this," the Duke said simply, without hint of a whine or supplication.

Six colored pictures of the Duke, locked to the plumbing in a cheap motel, began to fill up with detail. Dorfler grinned with satisfaction at his work, scooped them up, and slipped them in his pocket. He winked at the accountant, hunched on his knees on the bathroom floor and looking for the first time all week like he didn't know what to say. "Adios, Kemo Sabe," said Dorfler with a wink and a leer, turning and heading out.

The Duke did not protest or plead, but he winced when he heard the door slam. He sat down on the floor between the sink and the toilet. As he heard Dorfler drive away he tried to steady his breathing, but still sounded like somebody gasping in a whirlpool. He had spent five days trying not to think about his wife. No matter how hard he tried, he couldn't stop now. His eyes filled, and he propped his forehead against the cool of the sink. He was a man waiting to die.

11

WALSH'S EARS BARELY popped going up in the FBI Gulf-stream jet. After being at seven thousand feet in Flagstaff all day long, he'd begun to feel like a sherpa goatherd. They were barely airborne before Mosely and his three subs began to tap the bounty hunter for everything he knew. Walsh liked that, because he was as eager as they were. He knew there were things he couldn't change, like Gail, and he'd had to see her to let go of her. But he also knew it was time to reclaim something—his balls. Either that or hang it up.

About Mosely and his crew, Walsh saw that when these guys had an actual mission to plan—an outlet for their addiction to covertness—they weren't such jerks. Perry, who had been transcribing everything the bounty hunter said, turned to his chief for a qualification. "If he takes those disks, sir, even though they're blank . . . that's the overt act, correct?"

Mosely drew a breath to answer, and Walsh cut him off. "If he just sets *foot* in the airport, he's committed an overt act. Conspiracy to obstruct justice." Mosely nodded as Walsh spoke, almost as if he didn't take the interruption as an insult. For all his rage at the bounty hunter, days of it, he wasn't a petty man. His hunger for the big prize overrode everything else. Serano shimmered on the night horizon like a vision of justice triumphant. If Mosely could bring him in before morning, then the black man would be right up there with J. Edgar Hoover himself.

"If he shows up with the Duke," Walsh continued, "you can add kidnapping. If he shows up with anyone packing a gun, you can add conspiracy to commit murder." Walsh fairly glowed as he spoke. When he listed all the possible charges against Serano, it seemed a physical pressure lifted from his guts. His voice and his glittering eyes crackled with purpose and energy. "Now, the fact that it's an *airport*," he said, turning to face Mosely. "Alonso, correct me if I'm wrong here, but I think you could slap an ITAR rap on him." Interstate Travel in Aid of Racketeering—Walsh was up on all the fancy stuff. "With all that, you guys should be able to put him away for a couple thousand years."

The three subs were more than a little open-mouthed at the dazzle of Walsh's presentation. Mosely nodded with a sage half-smile, as if he couldn't have said it better himself. Agent Perry, not quite sure whose ass he ought to be kissing, leaned forward eagerly to the bounty hunter. "Yeah, but do you think he'll show?"

"Oh, he'll show," Walsh replied confidently, waving his empty coffee cup at Plumides, who jumped up to get the pot from the galley.

"Put a wire on him," said Mosely to Tuttle, and the bounty hunter nodded approval. It suddenly occurred to Walsh that maybe they were all just humoring him, because they thought he was going to die before morning. Walsh wasn't planning to die even a little bit, but it made him more than a little uncomfortable to think that opinion was running four to one.

•   •   •

When Dorfler pulled into the supermarket parking lot, his mood was almost giddy. He saw Tony and Joey waiting just where they said they'd be, by a row of soft-drink and candy machines. Tony slouched against the black Chrysler, while Joey rhythmically pounded an ice-cream machine that had eaten his quarter. It wasn't till Dorfler glided up and saw the two men up close that he thought about the incident in Amarillo. Tony had a puffed eye and a nasty welt on his cheek, and Joey's nose was twice its size.

Dorfler pulled up beside the Chrysler, and Tony sauntered around and leaned on the open driver's window. Before he could speak, Dorfler began to yap and smile at the same time, his words oozing out of a hard-set mask of obliging good will. "Hey, Tony, I'm real sorry about what happened back in Texas. You can imagine my extreme embarrassment when I found out who you were." He laughed in a fawning way, anxious to let bygones be bygones. "It's like I didn't even mean to hit you. It was, just one of those things, ya know? Like spur of the moment." Tony's face was utterly impassive, and Joey stood next to him now, his moron's mug as expressive as a dead man's. Dorfler arranged his face in a wheedling smile. "You guys know I'd never pull any shit like that."

"What the fuck took you?" asked Joey, scarfing his ice-cream sandwich.

"Yeah, well, I made a quick stop," replied Dorfler.

"Where is he?" Tony asked bluntly, a hand going into his jacket. He glanced in the back seat, then around the parking lot. Suddenly it was getting too complicated.

"Where's my money?" Dorfler countered, trying to sound suave and relaxed. But his mouth was very dry, and he could feel his heart in his ears.

"It's in the car. Where the fuck is he, Dorfler?"

"Yeah, well, there's been a slight change of plans,"

Dorfler replied, holding both hands tightly to the wheel to keep them still. "Now I'm gonna need *two* mill. See, I been readin' the papers," he said, beginning now to relax. Very soon people would learn to stop pushing Max Dorfler around. "This guy got you for fifteen mill. So I figure he's gotta be worth at least two to ya." He shook a scolding finger at Tony. "You can't play me for a chump, Tony."

Tony's nostrils flared, and his eyes got extremely shiny. He was barely holding back the rage. "How do we know you've got him?"

Dorfler smirked and reached proudly into his shirt pocket. He handed out the group of Polaroids to Tony, then laced his fingers together and felt the power surge in him. Sourly Tony went through the pictures, glaring at each one carefully as Joey peeked over his shoulder. "You gimme the million now," said Dorfler. "Then I call you in twenty minutes. Tell you where to drop off the *second* mill. Once I know it's there, I tell you where he is."

Tony continued to study the photos. Dorfler's laced fingers began to sweat a little, but it was mostly anticipation. He'd figured out all the angles. This was an airtight situation. Still, he wished Tony Daruvo would say something. "Simple, right?" asked the bounty hunter, maintaining his casual air at all costs. "Okay, Tony?"

Tony elbowed Joey aside. "Not okay," he retorted with a menacing gloat, pulling the .45 out of his pocket. Dorfler's face was a sudden mass of tics and confusion. There had to be some mistake here. "Nice try, asshole," said Tony, opening fire. Three bullets pumped into the bounty hunter's face and neck, flinging him back against the seat. An oozing ruby dribbled out of a smoky black circle in the center of his forehead. His laced fingers twiddled in a death spasm.

"What did you do *that* for?" asked Joey Ribuffo, jig-

gling the end of a finger in his ear to stop the ringing.
Neither man looked fearfully around for cops, since Vegas
cops didn't go out of their way to intrude on shootings in
parking lots.

"Look," said Tony, passing the Polaroids to the moron.
Even Joey Ribuffo saw them right away, the hand towels
hanging on the rack above the Duke's head. Each white
towel said *Golden Boy* in wrinkled green script. Tony
laughed softly and nudged Joey to look in the car. Dorfler's
toupee hung as if hinged to his scalp, and as Joey looked,
it slowly unpeeled itself and fell on the floor of the back
seat in a stunned little pile like a big, dead spider.

The punk-blond bodyguard helped Jimmy Serano into a
chinchilla-lined coat, as the boss talked past Sid Lyman to
a pair of goons. "I want ten of our best people," he
barked, "and I don't want any fuckups this time. As soon
as I get ahold of these friggin' disks, I want the both of
them dropped and flushed down the toilet."

As Serano talked, Sid Lyman paced in short, quick
steps, marking out a cramped, compulsive box in a corner
of the living room. "I don't think you should do this,
Jimmy," he said, shaking his head rapidly, no-no-no.

"Oh, you don't?" retorted Serano with rich sarcasm.
"And what do *you* propose I do?"

Sid Lyman faced Jimmy Serano in his best trial lawyer
stance. "Send Tony with a cash offer," he said. "Give
this guy whatever the hell he wants"—and he waved his
arm out the window at the lights of Vegas below, as if the
whole city was fair game for ransom—"but don't do
this."

Serano walked over to the floor-length, gold-marbled
mirror, stretched his pig's neck forward, and straightened
the knot in his Countess Mara tie. "Walsh ain't gonna take
money from me," he said, then laughed a short barracuda

bark. "He knows I'd come and get it an hour later. In his head, this is a clean trade. He gets what he wants, I get what I want." Jimmy Serano patted his wavy gray hair and strode to the door. "The guy's a friggin' burnout. He just wants his bounty money."

"Listen, Jimmy," protested Lyman, "as your lawyer I have to tell you—"

"Cool it, Sid," growled the big man, "or I'll squash *you* like a bug, too." And he swept into the elevator, attended by his three goons like a king about to pay a courtly visit.

A half minute later the entourage stepped out of the padded freight elevator into the bowels of the Starlight Casino garage. They moved with murderous purpose— almost in lock-step—toward Serano's silver, smoked-glass Lincoln stretch. The parking attendant who opened the door to the rear compartment wore the usual scarlet waist-coat with hollow gold buttons, making Serano seem even more like a puppet monarch. The goons let Serano go in first, then tumbled in after him like a bunch of linebackers.

The attendant stood aside as the limo rolled away. Then he ambled back to his cubicle, reached behind the wooden key-display board and pulled out a walkie-talkie. He pressed the call button. "They're coming your way," he said in a steely voice that made his uniform seem all the more ludicrous.

The Lincoln stretch pulled onto the Strip. Immediately a tan station wagon and a light blue sedan veered from the curb into traffic behind it. As the limo passed a cross street, another FBI car made a U-turn out of nowhere and fell into line. Within a quarter mile two more cars joined in. The feds looked like a brood of ducklings following the silver swan of the limo.

As the Gulfstream approached the lights of Vegas, Walsh

took the deepest breath he'd taken in years. There were times in his checkered career when he'd had a near sense of destiny about a bust coming down. He knew this meeting with Serano and the Duke would be one of those times, however it all came out. He stood up as Perry finished taping the receiver to the small of his back, then ran the tape wire around his waist and clipped the Vega mike to the inside of Walsh's shirt.

The bounty hunter tucked his shirt back in his pants and sat to strap his seat belt on. Across the way, Mosely stood at a bank of electronic equipment as dense and bewildering as the instrument panel in the cockpit. The black man leaned into a speakerphone and identified himself. The answer came abruptly, with scarcely any static at all: "Serano's left the casino and is heading west on Vegas Boulevard."

Mosely switched the speaker off without acknowledgment, and he turned to take his seat for the landing. As he belted himself in, he happened to lock eyes with Walsh. "What are *you* grinnin' about?" he asked the bounty hunter—but playfully. The migrainous edge had disappeared from his voice.

Walsh shrugged, but he didn't stop grinning. "I feel like a cop again," he said.

Mosely nodded and smiled shyly. He glanced up ahead to where the three subagents were strapped in next to the galley, staring blankly ahead like stooges. Mosely winked at the bounty hunter and gave him the thumbs-up sign.

The silver limo came around the curve at McCarran Airport, pulling to the curb and mooring itself in front of the Arrivals building. The three backfield bodyguards tumbled out and stood in a huddle by the open door, waiting. The black Chrysler was parked in a white zone across the median strip, but the airport police were not in the habit of tagging upscale cars, not in a town where the major white-collar job was gangster. As soon as they saw the goons pour out of the limo, Tony and Joey emerged from the Chrysler, dragging out the poor accountant.

The Duke was afraid beyond fear. His face was pale and clammy as a jellyfish, his nose and fingertips numb and icy cold. Yet the overdose of adrenaline that had ravaged him like a bolt of electric shock, ever since Dorfler left him in the *Golden Boy,* had left him weirdly detached. As Tony and Joey walked him across the median strip, he kept trying to separate the three goons and recall their names. One of them had brought him coffee once in Serano's suite and chatted about the Bears game. The Duke decided it wasn't appropriate to say hello.

Then all of a sudden he was facing Jimmy Serano, who stepped out of the silver Lincoln as they approached. The Duke and the king eyed each other at last. Though the accountant had been in the big man's suite several times, going over the books with Sid Lyman, he'd never been face to face with Serano himself. Just now he couldn't even remember ever seeing a picture of the gangster, though it must have been in the papers a hundred times. But the real thing was so much deadlier, so inescapably the end of the line, no wonder the horror seemed so new.

"So we finally meet," said Jimmy Serano, nodding up and down with a matinee-idol smile. "I'm in the presence of greatness." He looked around at his men and spread both arms in a gesture of theatrical humility. The goons laughed. "A Robin Hood who robs *hoods,*" said Serano, savoring the pun. "He takes from the scum of the earth and gives to the poor and downtrodden."

Tony Daruvo glanced around nervously, as if his radar had picked up the bevy of unmarked cars that cruised back and forth on the airport loop. "Listen, we better do this quick," he said, and Jimmy Serano shot him a savage look, that he would dare interrupt the king's speech. Tony avoided Serano's eyes as he quickly explained, "We had to pop Dorfler in a parking lot."

The Duke winced slightly, his face going a shade more livid, but Serano appeared to be completely uninterested in one more death. He drawled to the accountant, "Why don't you tell me all about these computer disks that Walsh is bringing?"

For a moment the Duke could hardly take it in, it was such a curve ball. Then he could feel the tension release in a tonic rush of hope. But he looked Serano straight in the eyes and silently dared him to notice. He spoke with a haughty cool worthy of his ducal station. "I was wondering when you were going to get around to that."

Walsh strode briskly from the docking gate into the voluptuous main terminal, with its great sweeps of window vaulting into the desert night. The bounty hunter looked as ragged and down-and-out as ever, his clothes battered and shapeless as if he lived on the street. His eyes scanned the crowded terminal. He was pleased to note that he couldn't pick out a single agent, though he knew there were several in place. No sign of Serano or the Duke, so he headed directly into the center of the bustling space, where he could wait like a sitting duck.

Serano's three goons entered through the main automatic doors, glancing at Walsh, then fanning out into the crowd. The bounty hunter affected not to notice, as he dug out the last Camel from the crumpled package in his shirt. He lit it with the leaky Zippo, the click of the lighter like a knock on wood. A half dozen more hit men of the linebacker variety were spreading out on the upper deck, taking positions so they could waste Walsh and the Duke a hundred different ways. Walsh looked lazily at his Timex, as if he was waiting for a ride to the suburbs.

Then he saw Serano come through the automatic doors, the Duke a half step behind him. Walsh took a long drag on the cigarette as the two men moved toward him. Serano wore a self-satisfied smile as lush as his chinchilla-lined coat. When the three men were face to face, he looked the bounty hunter up and down. "Well, Jack, I see you still spend all your money on clothes."

"You okay, Jonathan?" asked Walsh, ignoring the gangster.

"I'm all right," replied the accountant, his eyes moist as a basset hound's at the sight of Walsh. "They killed Dorfler."

Walsh made an involuntary sound, as if he'd taken a swift kick in the gut. Serano clucked with disdain. "You're still too serious, Jack."

Once more Walsh addressed the Duke, as if the big chinchilla weren't even there. "Get behind me, Jonathan." The Duke nodded and moved discreetly from his place beside Serano's shoulder. He stood behind Walsh's back like a second in a duel, staring nakedly at the gangster. Nothing intruded now between Walsh and Serano. All over the terminal the various hit men were riveted on the meeting. They all knew the back story of the bounty hunter and the gangster. They were here to make sure the story had a happy ending.

Serano laughed with coarse disdain. "Maybe if you and I had done business way back, Walsh, you wouldn't look like a guy with a cup in his hand." Walsh took the insult with cool indifference. Only the Duke saw the smallest ripple shiver across the bounty hunter's shoulder blades. "So, you got the disks?" asked Serano. "Or did you lose them, too . . . like your job?"

Walsh put a hand to the side pocket of his jacket, and fifteen hit men reached toward their shoulder holsters. Walsh drew four computer disks from the pocket and held them out to the gangster. It was Serano who wouldn't let the moment go. As if to tease the bounty hunter, he didn't take the offering right away, but let Walsh stand with his hand extended. "By the way," said the big man with a gelid smile, "I always meant to ask you, how did it feel to lose your wife to another cop?"

Walsh remained impassive, holding out the disks, till Serano realized it wasn't worth the trouble to torture a dead man. He took the disks from Walsh's hand and slipped them in the pocket of his tycoon's coat. Suddenly a smile like sunshine broke across Walsh's face. "You know, Serano," he said, "there's something I've been wanting to say to you for ten years."

Serano perked up to think they might be able to trade a few insults, after all. He could see the laugh lines crinkling Walsh's cheeks like pleating fabric. "Oh, yeah? What's that?"

"You're under arrest," replied Walsh with effortless calm.

And suddenly the air was alive with the clicking of guns, as if some vast slot machine were about to hit the jackpot. It seemed as if half the people wandering through the terminal were suddenly poised like killing machines, guns trained at Serano's head, covering every goon and hit man before they could get their own guns out of their holsters. The whole terminal fell utterly silent as every traveler froze on a dime.

Serano looked around, bewildered. His whole life had been a winning game where guns were pointed at *other* people. "What the fuck is this?" he said, genuinely confused.

Something about the dumb Brooklyn street way he said it struck Walsh as funny, profoundly funny, cosmically funny. Laughter began to gurgle from the deepest part of his being. "Forty to life," he said to the gangster, a chortle of merriment erupting from him like a burp.

Which started the Duke going. As a wave of feds descended on the indignant Serano, the cords of whose neck were strangled with rage, Walsh and the Duke seemed to melt in bottomless laughter, braying like jackasses. Maybe it was the lack of sleep, or the strain. They had to lean against each other to keep from falling down. They shrieked with delight as Serano was led away, and all his goons and bodyguards were herded to the doors.

Walsh wiped the tears from his eyes in time to see Mosely heading out with his prisoners. The black man turned and flashed a grin at Walsh, eager as a rookie, and the bounty hunter returned him the thumbs-up sign as the agent disappeared from the terminal. The Duke was still laughing fitfully, punch-drunk with relief. The pedestrian traffic in the terminal resumed its buzz and hectic pace, as if the whole thing had been nothing more than a fire drill.

The Duke laid a hand on Walsh's arm. "I'm very proud of you, Jack," he said. "I didn't mean it when I called you a coward. I was just trying to motivate you."

"No problem, Jonathan," Walsh replied with an easy smile, reaching into his back pocket and pulling out the handcuffs.

"What are you doing?" asked the Duke, shocked and alarmed, as the bounty hunter clicked the cuffs in place on the accountant's sore, red wrists.

"We still got two and a half hours to get you to L.A."

And he led the Duke away through a milling crowd of people with other places to go. Neither man made any attempt to hide the cuffs anymore. Walsh dragged him along by the cuff chain—like pulling an elephant by the trunk. But nobody seemed to pay them any notice, either. Perhaps the drama of Serano's arrest, the rounding up of his goons, was very hard to upstage. Jack Walsh and the Duke seemed like pretty small potatoes. You had to do better than handcuffs to entertain people used to shoot-outs and drug busts and serial killers, the gaudy Vegas floor show that lit the sky with neon.

Walsh and the Duke were both deep in thought as the 727 made its approach to L.A. The Duke looked down at the spider web of lights that pooled the valleys between the mountain ranges. To the accountant it felt as if the plane was being sucked into the web, and he himself was a helpless, paralyzed fly. Out of the corner of his eye he saw the bounty hunter check his trusty Timex. He was determined for once not to be the first to speak.

"When I took this job," said Walsh, "I figured I'd never make it. Not in a million years." He laughed, somewhere between a bark and a dry cough. "But for a hundred grand, I figured I had to give it a try." The Duke said nothing and seemed to hold back. Walsh had the curious feeling that the accountant wasn't buying any of what he just said. Jonathan Mardukas had somehow been the only man he'd met in years who thought Jack Walsh could do anything right. A prisoner who actually *believed* in his bounty hunter, for God's sake.

Walsh's voice grew suddenly mild. "If you had your way, what would you do? Where would you go?"

"Mexico," replied the Duke without a moment's pause. "I'd call Dana and have her collect whatever money we've got stashed. Then she'd fly down and meet me in Mazatlán." He paused for a moment, as if the vision of it were so intense he could touch it. He shook his head wistfully. "Nobody would bother us. We'd live well down there."

"Drinkin' margaritas while the sun goes down?"

"Every single night," the Duke replied gravely, then sank back into his seat and closed his eyes for landing. The bounty hunter said no more, recalling the Duke's respectful silence after the visit with Gail. Walsh stared out the window as the plane headed into LAX. A coastal fog nuzzled the streetlights. Walsh didn't know if the sinking feeling in his gut was related to the change of altitude or the pang that always attended coming home to a place where he was nothing. All he knew was that he felt awful.

Twenty minutes later, no luggage at all, Walsh and the Duke were riding the escalator down to the main exit. The accountant's hands hung limply before him, seized by the handcuffs. It was difficult to say who looked more tired, or who had the longer way to go. Goodwill itself would not have accepted any of their garments.

They came off the escalator and crossed to a bank of pay phones. Walsh patted all his pockets fruitlessly, then looked at the Duke, who nodded. The bounty hunter dug a hand in his prisoner's pocket and took out the plastic change holder. He extracted a final quarter from among a heap of pennies, dropped it in the slot, and dialed Moscone's number. It had hardly rung a millisecond before the bondsman grabbed it up himself. "Yeah, Eddie Moscone here," he said with obvious misery.

"Hey, Eddie," said Walsh, "where's Jerry?"

"Feds picked him up twenty minutes ago. Where the hell are you?"

Walsh grinned into the phone. "Me? I'm in L.A., of course. With the Duke. You want to say hello?" The Duke was staring disconsolately out at the airport traffic, realizing he was about to take his last ride. Suddenly Walsh put the phone to his ear, and he spoke with automatic politeness: "Hello, Mr. Moscone."

Then Walsh grabbed the phone back and crowed into it. "Now say good-bye, you lying piece of shit! Because I'm letting him go!" And he crashed the phone back on its hook, slapped his hands together, and let loose an exuberant yelp. The Duke was one step behind, too weary to follow another change of plans and another double cross. Who was Walsh going to turn him in to *now?*

But the bounty hunter slipped the key from his pocket and uncuffed the accountant's wrists. The Duke was so dazed that he continued to hold his hands together, as if he had internalized the bondage. Walsh clapped a hand on his shoulder. "May your footsteps be heard in heaven, your grace," he said, "before the devil knows you're gone."

"I don't get it," the Duke replied, wary as hell.

Walsh shrugged and flashed his patented half grin. "I did what I wanted to do," he said. "I got you to L.A. by midnight Friday." He shrugged again, almost as if embarrassed by the bald simplicity of it all.

The Duke stared at him deeply. He knew himself well enough to know he always felt a bit guilty when somebody did something nice for him. It was always so much easier to be nice to someone else. He'd finally given up trying to angle for his release. He'd resigned himself to his fate at last. In the first moment of freedom the freedom hurt, like starting all over again. "I don't know what to say," he replied shyly.

"Don't say anything," retorted the bounty hunter. "Get out of here before I change my mind."

Same old Jack, thought the Duke, echoing what Gail had said. God forbid anyone should discover the bounty hunter's deepest secret: Jack Walsh was a decent man. The accountant had always been right about people. This was the reward of so much openness, so many vitamins, hypnotherapy, deep massage, every de-stressing technique in the book. But just now the Duke did not bring up his marvelous instinct for character. All he said was: "Thanks, Jack. You're a really front-row guy."

"No, Jonathan—thank *you.*" With elaborate courtesy he shook the Duke's hand, a solid, affectionate grip, his other hand squeezing the Duke's shoulder. Then a curious antic look came into the bounty hunter's eye, and he dropped the Duke's hand and grabbed his wrist. A pang of misery swept the Duke's face as he flinched in anticipation of the handcuffs.

In a flash Walsh had cuffed him again . . . with the beat-up Timex. The Duke stared down at his wrist in startled disbelief. "So you'll remember our adventure," said Walsh, his voice as quiet as his grin.

A catch like an apricot pit stabbed the Duke's throat. He had to open his eyes wide and tilt his head back a little to keep the tears from spilling down his face. He looked down at the watch and stroked the crystal with the tip of one finger. "I'll treasure it," he said with feeling.

Then he unbuttoned his jacket. "I've got a gift for you, too, Jack." Now he unbuttoned the two middle buttons of his shirt. Walsh's forehead crinkled in confusion. There was a wide black belt under the Duke's shirt, like half a corset, which he now unhitched and pulled from around his waist. Walsh could see the zipper pattern on the Duke's belly from the underside of the belt. The accountant handed the belt over to the bounty hunter.

"Huh?" said Walsh, with eloquent understatement.

"When we first . . ." The Duke groped the air for the right word. ". . . *met*, I was packing to make my get-away. I figured the FBI was closing in." They both laughed. "So I took a little traveling money."

Walsh stared at the zipper that ran the whole length of the belt. In a sort of dream state—as if he didn't even realize anymore that he was standing in a public place— Walsh reached and tugged the zipper open a few inches. He saw currency packed as tightly as fat pads of note-paper. Thousand dollar bills. The warm, inky, crisp smell of new money instantly blessed his nostrils. "You son of a bitch," Walsh declared with a dazed smile.

"I told you I had money."

"I knew you had money, Jonathan. I didn't know you *had* money."

"It's not a payoff, Jack," the accountant added quickly, shaking his finger judiciously, as if he'd figured out the ethical part long ago. "You already let me go. This is a gift."

Walsh looked at the Duke for a long moment, then shook his head in wonder. "How much is here?"

"In the neighborhood of three hundred thousand."

"That's one of my favorite neighborhoods," murmured the bounty hunter, suddenly whipping his head around to check if anyone noticed the flash of green, as he zipped shut the money belt. But nobody paid them any mind, as people hustled to pick up their luggage or their grandmother. When he looked at the Duke again, they were both suddenly awkward, as if they'd run out of things to say.

The Duke cleared his throat. "Take care, Jack," he said. "If you're ever in Mazatlán . . ." His voice petered out, and he looked down. He knew Walsh never would. So did Walsh.

"Yeah, Jonathan, I'll look you up," he said, wanting this part to be over. He hated ritual good-byes, even if the feeling was real, *especially* if it was real. "Just get rid of that dog, huh?"

They were both grateful for a reason to laugh and move away from the obvious. They shook hands again, then Walsh closed his lips tightly, took a deep breath, turned, and walked away. The Duke thought he saw Walsh pause for an instant, maybe about to turn for another wave, but he kept walking, squaring his shoulders with a resolute jerk. The Duke headed back the way they'd come—to the phones, to Dana, to a thousand coral sunsets over the Sea of Cortez. He didn't see Walsh take one last backward look, just before the bounty hunter stepped out of the terminal.

Outside on the curb, Walsh took a contented look around him. A pretty girl with chestnut hair standing next to a white VW Rabbit waved at a young man next to Walsh. The man ran toward her with his one small suitcase, and they threw their arms about each other tightly. Walsh felt a pull in his chest, just a small one. He glanced at a clock over his head in a round glass bulb that hung at the end of a thin rod. It said 11:29.

"Thirty-one minutes to midnight, Walsh," he said to himself with satisfaction. "You would have made it."

Suddenly, he was starving. He walked over to the closest cab at the curb and leaned down to look at the driver. "You got change for a thousand?" he asked breezily.

The cabbie waved him off curtly. "Get outa here, you bum!"

Startled, Walsh looked down at himself. He'd forgotten how downright seedy he was in his grungy week-old duds. He swept his eyes up and down the exterior concrete corridor, wondering what to do first. One thing at a time. "Looks like I'm walking," he said with a smile, more to himself than the cabbie. Then he headed vaguely north along the sidewalk, toward the glittering city of last chances and a big, truckstop breakfast.